"Why are you afraid of falling in love?" Sylas asked.

"Who says I'm afraid?" Alana murmured, unable to answer his question honestly.

"You said you didn't want to kiss me because you didn't want to risk the consequences of falling in love with me. What are the grave consequences that frighten you so?"

Alana looked up at him. Her fingers curled; she could feel her nails making half-moons on her palms.

She hadn't told anyone, ever, what had happened to her or why she steered away from involvement. But she found herself wanting to tell Sylas.

Maybe it was because he was a good listener. Maybe it was because she had grown to trust him. Whatever her reasons, she knew now that she would never completely recover until she talked to someone....

But how would Sylas react?

Dear Reader,

Welcome to the Silhouette **Special Edition** experience! With your search for consistently satisfying reading in mind, every month the authors and editors of Silhouette **Special Edition** aim to offer you a stimulating blend of deep emotions and high romance.

The name Silhouette **Special Edition** and the distinctive arch on the cover represent a commitment—a commitment to bring you six sensitive, substantial novels each month. In the pages of a Silhouette **Special Edition**, compelling true-to-life characters face riveting emotional issues—and come out winners. All the authors in the series strive for depth, vividness and warmth in writing these stories of living and loving in today's world.

The result, we hope, is romance you can believe in. Deeply emotional, richly romantic, infinitely rewarding—that's the Silhouette **Special Edition** experience. Come share it with us—six times a month!

From all the authors and editors of Silhouette **Special Edition**,

Best wishes,

Leslie Kazanjian,
Senior Editor

JO ANN ALGERMISSEN
Best
Man

Silhouette Special Edition

Published by Silhouette Books New York

America's Publisher of Contemporary Romance

Books by Jo Ann Algermissen

Silhouette Desire

Naughty, but Nice #246
Challenge the Fates #276
Serendipity Samantha #300
Hank's Woman #318
Made in America #361
Lucky Lady #409
Butterfly #486
Bedside Manner #539
Sunshine #559

Silhouette Special Edition

Purple Diamonds #374
Blue Emeralds #455
Paper Stars #542
Best Man #607

JO ANN ALGERMISSEN

lives near the Atlantic Ocean, where she spends hours daydreaming to her heart's content. She remembers that as a youngster she always had "daydreams in class" written on every report card. But she also follows the writer's creed: write what you know about. After twenty-five years of marriage, she has experienced love—how it is, how it can be, and how it ought to be. Mrs. Algermissen has also written under a romanticized version of her maiden name, Anna Hudson.

Chapter One

"Wanna play pirates and make a treasure map?"

For an instant Alana Benton thought a child had dialed the wrong phone number. Then she recognized her childhood friend's voice. "Leslie Faye? Leslie Faye Hale?"

"Wrong response, Alana. You're supposed to say—"

"I'll loot my mom's jewelry box," Alana supplied, grinning as she recalled the incident. They'd both been seven years old then, and perpetually into mischief.

"Remember the oath we took that day?"

Twenty-three years should have dimmed the memory of two children nicking their thumbs and smearing their blood together, but Alana remembered it as though it had happened yesterday. "Best friends, forever and ever and ever."

"I thought you'd forgotten."

Alana twisted the telephone cord around her fore-finger, watching the way her pale skin turned a rosy pink. In the past decade, she thought guiltily, she hadn't been the best of friends to anyone. There had been a time when the "gruesome twosome," as their mothers had called them, had shared everything from doll clothes to boys' phone numbers. Although there had been occasional angry spats, they'd always ended with one of them falling into the other's arms and begging forgiveness.

For an instant Alana felt as though she should apologize now. She had to remind herself that they hadn't argued; they'd simply grown apart.

"So how are you, Leslie Faye?" she asked, sitting down on the edge of the bed she'd been about to make.

She hadn't heard from Leslie Faye since her last phone call a year ago, just after she'd filed for divorce. Since then, Alana's mother had kept her posted on Galveston's prime topic of local gossip: Leslie Faye Hale, gay divorcée.

"I've been better," Leslie Faye hedged. "I've been trying to call you for weeks. Have you been out of town on business?"

"Yeah. I'm just back from Wyoming."

"Cowboys and Indians in the courtroom?"

"More or less. A civil rights attorney I've worked with previously represented a Native American who'd been charged with armed robbery. Jury selection was tough, but more than likely it will turn out to be a case of mistaken identity."

"Gregory says it's illegal to rig a jury."

Alana opened her mouth to defend her job as a jury consultant, but Leslie Faye, apparently realizing she'd probably antagonized the person she'd called to ask a favor, quickly added, "Since practicing law is his all-consuming passion, Gregory doesn't think he needs a jury consultant any more than he thought he needed a wife. His partner, Sylas Kincaid, is handling my case."

"Your case?" Alana probed, thoroughly surprised. Her friend was known for having a heavy foot on the gas pedal of her car, but speeding tickets seldom warranted legal counsel.

"That's why I called you." Leslie Faye's voice dropped to a hushed whisper. "I've been ch-charged with assault and battery, with intent to do great b-bodily harm."

Alana unwound the telephone cord from her finger and pushed her dark, shoulder-length hair back from her face. Leslie Faye had always stammered when under tremendous stress. Alana held the phone receiver more firmly against her ear.

A mental picture of Leslie Faye formed as Alana closed her eyes. Stretched on tiptoe Leslie Faye barely reached the five-foot mark. At most, she weighed one hundred pounds. Her curly blond hair and rounded blue eyes completed the wholesome image. Nobody in their right mind would even contemplate the notion that she was capable of assault and battery.

Ridiculous, Alana silently scoffed, utterly ridiculous. A juror would have to be blind to find Leslie Faye guilty of that charge. And since she was from one of the oldest families on Galveston Island, it amazed Alana that Seth Hogan had allowed charges to be pressed against Leslie Faye at all.

"Alana? Are you there?"

"Yeah. I was wondering if the prosecuting attorney has gone senile. You're the last person Seth Hogan would want to appear on the witness stand."

"Seth retired. Avery Collier was appointed as the new prosecuting attorney."

"Oh?" She searched her memory, but came up blank. "An outsider?"

"Uh-huh. Gregory says Collier is taking every case to trial to build a tough law-and-order reputation. Anyone who files charges has his day in court."

Alana nodded and grimaced. She hated to risk offending her old friend by asking the next question, but she had to know the truth. Neither Leslie Faye's friendship nor her size made her automatically innocent of the charges filed.

"Did you physically assault someone?"

Leslie Faye paused. "Y-yeah, I guess I did. B-but honestly, Alana, I don't think I m-meant to hurt him."

Her muffled tone and her use of the word *honestly* warned Alana to be alert. Usually when people started a sentence with "honestly," or "frankly," or "to be truthful," they were lying through their teeth. She wished she could see her friend's face. Did her voice sound smothered because her hand was covering her mouth?

"Take a deep breath and calm down, Leslie Faye. Tell me exactly what happened."

"It's too awful to talk about on the phone," Leslie Faye protested. Her voice shook with desperation as it raised to a shrill pitch. "I'm in bad trouble. I know you're probably busy on another case, but you're my closest, dearest friend. You've got to help me. Please, come home!"

Although hysteria edged Leslie Faye's plea, Alana shook her head, biting her lip to keep from hastily saying yes. There had been many a night she'd fallen asleep with her pillow damp from tears of homesickness, but she'd vowed never to step foot in Galveston again, regardless of the circumstances.

As though Alana's negative thoughts trickled across the telephone wires, Leslie Faye badgered, "You can't say no, Alana. I know you're busy. I know I'm probably interrupting your schedule, but don't you understand? Avery Collier and Ed Morgan are going to lock me up in prison and throw away the key!"

"I haven't said I won't help you. I know two or three jury consultants in the Houston area who can help you."

Leslie Faye groaned aloud. "I need you, a friend, somebody who knows me, who believes in me."

Feeling as frustrated as a toddler kicking her heels on a concrete floor, Alana clenched the telephone receiver tightly, swallowed, then blurted, "I'll catch the first flight into Hobby Airport."

"You will?"

"Don't sound so surprised. We *are* friends."

After giving an audible sigh of relief, Leslie Faye said, "I knew you were the one person I could count on. There's a three o'clock flight from St. Louis to Houston on Delta. I made reservations for you. Okay?"

Alana chuckled. Her friend's diminutive size and Southern magnolia mannerisms made everyone wonder if the woman had a brain in her head or an ounce of gumption in her entire body, but she should have remembered that Leslie Faye could be a veritable human steamroller when she made up her mind to get something accomplished. Considering that most of the time Leslie Faye had been the one cajoling Alana into taking part in pranks Leslie Faye had thought up, she should have recalled how convincing her friend could be.

Of all people, who had learned better than Alana that outward appearances were deceptive? Her livelihood depended on accurately reading a person's body language. If she'd been standing toe-to-toe with her friend, she'd have known by the thrust of Leslie Faye's chin that she was determined to get her way.

"Okay. I'll throw some clothes in a suitcase and catch that flight."

"Spring clothes. It's already starting to get hot here. Don't worry about packing accessories. I'll take care of them for you."

"You always were the happy shopper, weren't you?" Alana said dryly.

Leslie Faye's mercurial temperament hadn't changed, Alana mused. One minute she could be so far down in the dumps a dredger couldn't locate her, and the next she'd be winging from cloud to cloud.

Leslie Faye giggled. "From shopper to shop owner! Would you believe I've opened a shop specializing in women's accessories?"

"You?"

When they were teenagers Alana was the one who'd wanted the career—who had vacillated between being the first woman astronaut and the first woman President. Leslie Faye admired Jacqueline Kennedy and Lady Bird Johnson. She wanted a husband—preferably a man interested in politics—a turn-of-the-century house on Galveston Island and scads of children. In that precise order.

Time and circumstances had altered the ambition of them both.

"Me!" Leslie Faye chortled, her voice laced with pride. "After I divorced Gregory I had to have something to do or I'd have gone crazy. When my charge cards reached their limit from shopping sprees, I decided I'd better get my act together before I completely exhausted my trust fund." Her voice changed. "I was starting to cope with my situation when this thing with Ed Morgan happened. Gregory says my reputation as a flamboyant party girl won't help my case."

"Never mind what your ex-husband says." Alana wanted to end their conversation on a upbeat note. Once she reached Galveston she'd make it her first task to stop Gregory from voicing his denigrating opinions. "If I'm going to be on that flight, I'm going to have to get a move on."

"I can hardly wait to see you! It's been too long, Alana, way too long. We have a lot of catching up to do."

"I've missed you, too." She hadn't realized how much until she'd heard her friend's voice. Despite Leslie Faye's being in trouble and Alana's vow to permanently shake the Galveston Island sand from her boots, she found she was actually looking forward to returning home. "I'll see you this afternoon. Bye."

"Wait a second!"

"Yes?"

"Alana...thanks. I don't know why you hightailed it out of Texas, but I can't tell you how much I appreciate your coming back to help me."

The sincerity in Leslie Faye's voice brought a nostalgic ache to the back of Alana's throat. She had difficulty swallowing past the emotional knot. Her voice was low and husky when she replied, "Me, too."

As she replaced the phone in its cradle, she knew she didn't regret transferring from Texas A and M University to Stephens College during her sophomore year. Under the circumstances, Alana believed that transferring to a college where the women outnumbered the men ten to one was truly the only choice she could make to save her sanity. But she had regretted leaving her parents, her friends, her home.

Leslie Faye wasn't the only one who'd wondered why Alana hadn't come home. The first summer she'd stayed in Missouri, on the pretext of going to summer school to make up the credits she'd lost by transferring, her parents had been patient with her. The following Christmas, when she told them she had term papers to write, they'd come to visit her. Spring vacation the three of them had gone to Florida. Gradually her parents had accepted the fact that she'd made a new life for herself apart from them.

Her mother had made several references in her letters to the difficulty of adjusting to the empty nest syndrome, but her father had filled the empty space by purchasing several acres of land in the hill country. Overseeing the clearing of the land and the building of a house, and choosing new furnishings, not to mention her usual social functions, had kept her mother busy.

After Alana graduated and began working as a jury consultant, excuses came easily. Since she traveled forty or more weeks out of the year, her parents believed her when she told them she preferred to have them visit her. Her father's retiring and their move made it even easier for her to avoid Galveston. Her parents had made a new home for themselves and she'd made a life for herself outside of Texas.

She'd never told them why she left, either.

After she dealt with Leslie Faye's problem, she just might pay them an unexpected visit. The frequent letters they wrote weren't a great substitute for one of her father's bear hugs or one of her mother's smiles.

Ten years, she mused. Where had they gone? Had it taken a decade to recover from the emotional blow she'd sustained?

"I'm well and happy," she said, practicing the positive thinking that started and ended each of her days. Honestly, she hadn't had a nightmare for months.

Alana grimaced as she shifted her weight to straighten the coverlet on her bed. Her thought had begun with a cue word—honestly. Leslie Faye wasn't the only person who started a sentence with a word like *honestly* when she was about to tell a lie. Alana couldn't lie to herself. It *had* been months since she'd awakened with her heart pounding, in a cold sweat that made her sheets stick to her skin. But a day never passed when she wasn't careful not to get herself into a stupid situation, one beyond her control.

A tremor ran through her hands as she fluffed her pillow. She could feel her face getting hot. With careful deliberation, Alana straightened, crossed to the mirror hanging over her dresser and pointed at her reflection.

"Don't think about it. It won't happen again, that's for damned certain. Leslie Faye would have helped you if you'd been able to tell her what happened. She's called you, asking for your help. You're going to go there, make certain she gets a fair trial and then get on with your life. This isn't forever—only temporary."

She glanced at the bed she'd just made, then tore off
the coverlet and stripped the bed of its sheets. She'd
welcome the feel of clean linen after she finished her
work in Texas. Crossing to the bathroom, she folded
the soiled sheets and placed them in the dirty clothes
hamper. She chose clean pale green bed linens, which
perfectly matched the serene green in the draperies.
Swiftly, efficiently, she remade the bed, careful to fold
the bottom corners neatly, securely. She hated a slop-
pily made bed.

Before she started to pack, she decided she'd better
call her answering service to inform them of her
change of plans.

"Leslie Faye's luck isn't all bad," she muttered as
she dialed the number. "If she'd called a week later,
I'd have been in Washington."

"Benton Consultant Services."

"Susan, this is Alana. Any calls for me?" She heard
Susan chuckle. "What's so funny?"

"I just made a bet with Lorna that you'd be antsy
to start a new case and that you'd call here before ten
o'clock to check the schedule."

Alana shrugged. "What can I say? I like my work."

"All work and no play..." Susan chided, letting the
truism dangle without completing it.

"Makes me deliriously happy," Alana finished.
"My schedule is clear except for the Kelin case in Se-
attle, right?"

Susan's voice lost the hint of laughter as she replied, "Correct."

"I've been contacted by a friend who's asked me to
work on a case in Galveston, Texas. I'm leaving this
afternoon. Once I get there, I'll call to give you a
number where I can be reached."

"Isn't Galveston near Houston? Home of the As-
tros, Cotton-Eyed Joe and magnificent urban cowboys? Could you bring back a souvenir? Preferably a
cowboy?"

Alana silently groaned. Susan invariably romanticized every city on Alana's agenda. She'd tried over
the years of their association to convince her that she
seldom saw more than the inside of her hotel suite and
the courthouse of the city where she worked, but Susan was incorrigible.

"Kidnapping is a felony," Alana quipped.

"Who said anything about kidnapping?" Susan
joked. "Lure him into your hotel room and promise
him wild, glorious sex."

Alana's fingers tightened on the telephone. Like
Leslie Faye, Susan was outrageously outspoken. She
had no idea that her innocent remarks pricked Alana
like thorns under a saddle blanket.

Don't be oversensitive, she scolded herself, consciously loosening her tight grip on the phone.

"Dream on, Susan. That's about as close as I'll
come to one of your cowboys. I'll touch base with you
soon," she concluded. "Bye."

Alana made a check mark on her mental list of
things to do before she left St. Louis, and began pac-
ing herself to get everything accomplished and make
it to the airport an hour before departure. She automatically reached down and unplugged her clock and
the bedside lamp. She seldom took risks, even with
something as remote as an electrical fire.

She crossed her bedroom to the walk-in closet. Methodically, she chose attire appropriate for the cli-
mate and her profession. Before she hung her suits and
blouses in the garment bag, she checked each piece of

clothing for spots. The dry cleaner where she'd taken them was speedy and convenient to her condo, but none of the employees had her eye for perfection.

She hadn't realized how much the idea of returning to Galveston was affecting her until she stood at the front door of her condo ready to depart. She'd gone through the routine of straightening her belongings hundreds of times, but this time as she put her key in the dead-bolt lock an ominous feeling threatened to consume her.

With a twist of her wrist, she locked the door. It isn't as though I'm running away this time, she mused. And it isn't as though anyone in Texas knows why I left there.

"I'll be back," she promised herself aloud, feeling ridiculous for letting the prospect of a short trip to Texas shake her equilibrium. She straightened her shoulders, cautiously glancing from left to right, then lifted her suitcase and marched toward her car.

"You don't need a blasted jury consultant!"

Sylas Kincaid raised one dark eyebrow as he pondered Gregory's vehement objections to having Alana Benton work on the case. Sylas leaned forward, pointing to the article in *Significant People* magazine that featured the woman his law partner obviously disliked.

"I've never worked with a consultant. It should be educational."

"Educational? Disastrous!" Gregory injected. "She'll upset Leslie Faye."

Sylas folded his hands in the center of his desk, leaned forward slightly and prepared to listen to Gregory. "How?"

"How?" Gregory jumped to his feet. "She's a publicity hound! You read the articles about her. Alana Benton is one of those liberated female types. When Leslie Faye and Alana were kids, do you know what Alana wanted to be when she grew up?"

"What did she want to be?" Sylas asked politely.

"The first woman President of the United States! Doesn't that tell you something?"

Sylas grinned, glancing at the attractive woman in the picture. "She has a few more years to start her campaign," he quipped. "She isn't thirty-five yet, is she?"

Gregory tossed a quelling glare over his shoulder and strode to the window. Outside a storm brewed. A northern wind whipped the water until whitecaps dotted the Gulf's surface.

"If we're lucky this storm will develop into a hurricane and they'll shut down the airport," he grumbled. "You'll have to take my word on this. Alana Benton is a bad influence. She always stuffed my wife's head with foolish nonsense."

"Ex-wife," Sylas corrected.

"Yeah. I'll bet Alana Benton had something to do with ruining my marriage, too." His hands clenched into fists; he shoved them in his trouser pockets. "God knows Leslie Faye didn't have grounds. I gave her everything a woman could ask for—a nice house, new car, charge cards at her favorite stores. All I expected in return was for her to welcome me home with open arms, to have a decent meal on the table and clean sheets on the bed. I think that's a fair exchange for my working my butt off at the county courthouse, don't you?"

"It's a little late to be asking my opinion. A year ago I tried to offer a few suggestions and you told me confirmed bachelors shouldn't offer marital advice. You said—"

Gregory sliced his hand through the air and barked, "Don't remind me. I know what I said. The mere thought of Leslie Faye crying out the intimate details of our marriage on your shoulder—after she had the nerve to toss out my clothes on the front lawn and set fire to them—made me see red. I don't know what it is that makes women feel they can pour out their hearts to you, but they do. It's no wonder you're the best damned divorce lawyer in Galveston."

Sylas got to his feet and crossed to stand beside Gregory. "I'd have felt a hell of a lot more comfortable representing her for a divorce than I do in a criminal case. And from the articles I've read about Alana Benton, her helping with jury selection may give me the edge I need to win the case."

"Bull! You don't need her to rig the jury. Just put twelve women in the jury box and Ed Morgan doesn't have a prayer."

"Avery Collier isn't going to allow that to happen. He can red-line as many potential jurors as I can."

"I'm telling you, you don't need Alana's help. She's nothing but a glory hound. She'll probably bring a camera crew and a writer from some slick magazine to do a sensationalized story about this case. Think of what that will do to Leslie Faye." Gregory shook his head decisively, his chin thrust forward. "Don't bother trying to convince me you need Alana Benton by saying you're a civil, not a criminal, attorney. You know Texas law inside out. Other than myself, you're the best man to represent Leslie Faye."

"Thanks for the vote of confidence, but it doesn't change the facts. I can use all the help I can get."

Sylas knew why doubts were gnawing at his self-confidence. Give him a hot civil suit and seven times out of ten his research and powers of persuasion would sway the jury toward his client's claim. But this case worried him. He'd spent long days and nights doing research on Leslie Faye's behalf, but he genuinely feared that the minute the twelve jurors saw the scar running down the side of Ed Morgan's face, Leslie Faye's plea of self-defense would be in serious trouble.

"She trusts you. I trust you." Gregory clamped his hand on his partner's shoulder. "I wish she didn't trust Alana."

"Have you expressed your opinion to her?"

"Repeatedly. Each time she placed a call to St. Louis and moaned and groaned about getting Alana's telephone recorder, I told her that perhaps it was better if Alana was unavailable. Then she'd begin telling Alana-saves-the-day-for-Leslie-Faye history lessons." He raked his fingers across his jaw. "Quite pointedly she said that Alana has always been there when she really needed her. What the hell do you think she was implying by that remark?"

"Gregory, sometimes you're like a coonhound barking up the wrong tree. If you want to know exactly what she meant, ask her to tell you, not me."

From the tidbits of information Gregory had reluctantly revealed to Sylas on previous occasions, Sylas strongly suspected lack of communication had contributed to the breakup of Gregory's marriage.

"I didn't have to ask," Gregory mumbled. "She thinks *I* should have taken her case. I told her surgeons don't operate on relatives and lawyers don't represent their *ex*-wives.''

On ethical grounds, Sylas agreed with Gregory, but he wondered how Leslie Faye had reacted. "What did she say?''

"She looked at me as though I had bananas in my ears, picked up the phone and redialed Alana's number. I'm telling you, Alana is a bad influence. I don't want her within a thousand miles of Galveston.''

Sylas glanced at his watch. "Since she arrived at the airport ten minutes ago, and we're supposed to meet them at Leslie Faye's condo, I'd say the question is moot.''

"Not yet." Gregory clapped Sylas on the back then rubbed his hands together. "I want you to bluntly inform Alana Benton that you don't want her on the case.''

"Is that an order?''

"A friendly request." Gregory lifted his head to meet Sylas eye-to-eye. "Trust me. I know what's best for Leslie Faye.''

Alana stepped from the corridor that connected the plane to the waiting room. During the flight she'd had several panic-stricken moments when she'd had to take deep breaths and silently reassure herself that no one in Galveston knew why she'd left. No one would be standing at the airport pointing a finger at her. No one would give her sly, speculative looks. Her secret had been kept safely locked inside of her.

"Yoo-hoo! Over here!" Leslie Faye called, using her sharp elbows to weave her way among the people—giants compared to her—who were competing with her for space.

Alana grinned from ear to ear, dropped her attaché case and opened her arms as Leslie Faye catapulted against her.

"You can still give one hell of a bear hug," she said, chuckling as she stepped back to take a long look at her friend.

Leslie Faye hadn't grown an inch or gained a pound. Her brightly colored scarf and shoulder-length earrings bore witness to her present occupation as owner of an exclusive accessory shop. Only a person who knew Leslie Faye was under stress would have noticed the purple smudges under her eyes, artfully covered with makeup. "You look great!"

"You look...fit, but then I always did envy the way you could wear a flour sack and manage to look chic."

The backhanded compliment would have annoyed Alana if she hadn't grown up with Leslie Faye. She hadn't changed one iota. Alana had often teased her friend about having been assembled in heaven without a filter between her brain and her mouth. Whatever Leslie Faye thought, Leslie Faye said.

Alana's grape-colored suit and low-heeled shoes suited the professional image she wished to project. Wearing conservative clothing, she could blend into a crowd without being noticed. She wasn't here for a fun-filled vacation or a frivolous reunion with her friend. She was here on business, serious business. She'd planned her wardrobe accordingly.

"Not to worry," Leslie Faye blithely said. "You take care of my problem and I'll put you back on the plane to St. Louis looking as though you spent a wad of money at Neiman Marcus. Come on, we'll get your suitcases. I'll have to drive like crazy to get to the

Causeway before the five o'clock traffic jams the highway.''

''Why don't we stop in Clear Lake City for dinner at Frenchie's? It'll give us a chance to talk about your case and we won't have to be bothered with fixing dinner.''

''I've got a pot roast in the oven,'' Leslie Faye replied with a hesitant smile. ''I knew you'd want to get down to the legal technicalities on the case, so I invited Gregory and Sylas to join us.''

Wishing she had been consulted before those plans were made, Alana said, ''Then we'll have to talk about what happened on the drive back to Galveston.''

''Can't it wait? Gregory and Sylas know the gory details. Can't they tell you what happened after dinner while I load the dishwasher?''

Alana disliked the idea of getting down to the "gory details" of the case the moment she'd stepped off the plane as much as Leslie Faye did. Aware of her friend's ploy to avoid unpleasantness for as long as possible, Alana knew she'd have to be firm.

Ideally, they'd have shared the first night after a lengthy separation in an adult version of their teenage sleep-overs; they'd have talked until the wee hours of the morning about everything and nothing.

But this wasn't an ideal situation.

While she mulled over an answer, Leslie Faye tucked her small hand into the crook of Alana's arm. ''But I'm so happy you're here. I don't want to spoil your homecoming by going through what happened.''

They could have postponed this until morning, Alana mused, if the attorneys had not been invited to dinner. This forced her to be candid with Leslie Faye.

"I'm glad to be with you, too, but you're going to have to tell me what happened. We both know I'm not your ex-husband's favorite person. Won't I look like a foolish ninny exchanging polite chitchat when he knows I'm here to work on the case?"

Leslie Faye ducked her head and mumbled something, but over the hubbub in the airport Alana didn't hear her. "What'd you say?"

"Gregory thinks Sylas can win the case without you."

"What do you think?"

For several seconds, while Alana presented her claim check to the attendant and they walked to the luggage carousel, Leslie Faye thoughtfully formulated her response. Alana noticed her friend's hands twisting the shoulder strap of her purse.

"Gregory trusts Sylas. I trust him, too. But I don't want to leave anything to chance. I don't have proof of what happened that night. It's purely my word against Ed's. H-he lied to the police. They believed him. I'm the one who was b-booked."

Tears gathering in her eyes, Leslie Faye cleared her throat to regain her composure. "There's a chance the jury might believe him, too. From what I've read about you and your job, your being there when the jury is selected can make a difference in the final outcome." She raised her chin defiantly. "I don't want to go to jail for defending myself. Ed Morgan is the one who ought to be on trial, worrying about going to prison."

"What charge?"

"Attempted rape," Leslie Fay whispered.

Alana's eyes had been watching the revolving belt for her suitcases; now they circled within easy reach, but her arms wouldn't move. Her back stiffened as though she'd taken a killing blow. The breath she'd inhaled seemed to explode in her lungs. Black spots spiraled before her eyes. Light-headed and dizzy, she felt her knees turned to water.

"Alana!" Leslie Faye grabbed her around the waist. "Dear God, don't faint. Help! Somebody help me!"

Chapter Two

Somebody help me! Alana silently screamed into the dark oblivion swallowing her. Her eyelids fluttered as she struggled against falling into the hellish nightmare about to envelop her.

"Put her head between her knees," a gray-haired woman with the voice of a drill sergeant ordered as she helped Leslie Faye support Alana's limp body. "Don't panic. I'm a nurse."

"Is she going to be okay?" Leslie Faye dropped to her knees. Scared, she babbled, "One minute we were standing here talking and the next minute Alana crumpled toward the ground."

"Breathe deeply, Alana, slowly," the stranger instructed. "That's good. Slowly, in...out...in...out."

No! Alana mouthed. Stop it! Eyes squeezed shut, she flailed blindly with her hands into the empty space in front of her. Stop it!

Leslie Faye lunged forward to wrap her arms around Alana's shoulders and neck. "Is she going to die? Should I get to a phone and call an ambulance?"

"Move back. Give her some air." The woman addressed Leslie Faye and the horde of curious people who'd begun to form a tight circle around them. "She doesn't need an ambulance and she isn't going to die. This sometimes happens when a passenger leaves a pressurized aircraft. It could have been something she ate. It's nothing to get excited about. She'll be fine."

Alana fought her way out of the nightmare by chanting silently, This isn't real. It isn't happening to me. I'm going to open my eyes and it will be all over. This isn't real. It isn't happening to me.

Her eyelids felt as though they were weighted as she pried them open. She brushed her hands down the length of her suit jacket, then tugged at her dress hem, which had hiked up above her knees.

A sigh escaped her parted lips. It wasn't Tom holding her head in a death grip. It was her friend. Her dear, dear friend. A single tear slid from the corner of her eye as she remembered Leslie Faye's last word . . . *rape*.

"Leslie Faye, I'm sorry. I'm so very, very sorry."

"Don't be an idiot! You didn't make a spectacle of yourself on purpose. You should know you can't embarrass me." She brushed Alana's bangs off her forehead. "I'll admit you did scare ten years' growth from me. Are you okay?"

"No . . . I mean, yes. I'll survive."

A red tide of humiliation tinged her cheeks as she turned her head. Legs, like a semicircle of courthouse pillars, surrounded her. Mortified at having made a scene in public, she lurched to her knees in an attempt to scramble to her feet.

She held on tightly to Leslie Faye's arm. "For heaven's sake, get me out of here," she whispered. "Everybody is staring at me."

"See?" The nurse beamed Leslie Faye a smile that wreathed her face in a web of tiny wrinkles. "Delayed airsickness is what I call it. Don't drink and fly, otherwise you'll have to crawl to a taxicab."

Alana inwardly groaned at the woman's mild rebuke. She hadn't had an alcoholic beverage, but she preferred to let Leslie Faye think that she had than explain why she'd fainted.

"Thank you for your help," Leslie Faye said, a thread of haughtiness edging her voice. She helped Alana to her feet, glancing toward the carousel. "You lean against this rail. There are two gray suitcases over there. Are they yours?"

Alana nodded, swallowing hard to calm her stomach. Her mind raced as she tried to decide what explanation to give Leslie Faye. Should she tell her the truth?

"I'll be right back. Don't move a muscle."

Again, Alana nodded. Unfortunately, she wasn't going anywhere. She'd have signed over her portfolio of stocks and bonds for a ticket on the next departing flight. Before Leslie Faye returned with her suitcases she'd have to get a grip on herself.

How could she bear to listen to her friend recount what had happened to her? Just the thought of rape was enough to make her stomach heave.

She'd already made one scene. She simply couldn't disgrace herself further by throwing up. The few

stragglers remaining in the area would think she was
dead drunk.

Maybe she should stop Leslie Faye from getting her
suitcases. She had a perfectly legitimate excuse to
leave: Gregory didn't want her on the case.

Dammit, Benton, you can't let him ride roughshod
over her, over you. And you can't disappoint her
again. What's left of your friendship would be totally
shattered. Leslie Faye would think you didn't care
enough to stand up to him. Stop being such a god-
damned coward.

She leaned heavily against the rail, allowing her
hand to graze across her stomach, then raising it until
her palm rocked against her forehead and her fingers
splayed through her bangs. Think!

"You wait right there while I find somebody to help
with the luggage. You'll feel better once you're outside in the fresh air," Leslie Faye said. Attempting to
bring the normal color back into Alana's face, she
added, "If I can't find anyone, I'll give you a ride on
one of the suitcases."

Alana made an honest effort to smile, but her lips
were frozen into a grim straight line. She'd made a
complete ass out of herself. Far worse, she couldn't
explain her reaction to what Leslie Faye had revealed
without exposing the story she had hidden so carefully all these years.

Leslie Faye had more than her share of problems
without burdening her with how stupid Alana had
been nine years ago.

Perplexed and heartsick, Alana tugged at the short
dark hair that feathered back from her face. Rape. At
the thought, nausea almost overcame her. Rape was
the one type of case she refused to accept. After once

watching a talk show host interviewing rape victims on national television, she'd completely avoided ever again reading about, viewing or discussing the subject.

While the audience had oohed and aahed with sympathy, Alana had studied their body language. More than half the people gushing commiseration with the victims couldn't disguise their real attitudes. Eyes narrowed in speculation; raised eyebrows; feet tapping with impatience. One woman had steepled her fingers over her ample bosom as though she'd appointed herself judge and jury.

Alana had known what they were thinking. Nice girls don't get raped. They must have done something to push the men beyond control. They'd asked for it. One poor woman on the show mistakenly admitted having a couple of beers. The audience had practically crucified her.

Alana seriously doubted if those attitudes had changed during the past decade, especially here in good-ol'-boy Texas. The absurd double standard, where men were expected to be studs and women were expected to be virtuous, remained the unwritten law. While "boys would be boys," women were "good" or "bad." A woman with loose morals got what she deserved.

Alana had been raised with those beliefs; so had her friend.

Leslie Faye hadn't exaggerated. She was in big trouble. Half the jurors would be prejudiced against her before the prosecuting attorney opened his mouth.

Alana couldn't let that happen. She wouldn't let that happen. How could she look at herself in the mirror each morning if she was too gutless to defend her friend?

Without realizing it, Alana had straightened her shoulders. Her hands had settled on her hips as though she were a wild West gunfighter ready to take on a band of pistol-packing bad guys. Her stomach continued to feel as though it was tied in knots, but she was used to the nervous symptoms related to facing a difficult challenge.

She'd keep her secret, she decided silently. It was too late to seek justice for herself through the legal system, but it would give her great satisfaction to know she'd helped seek justice on Leslie Faye's behalf.

Leslie Faye was the victim, not the man who'd had her arrested. When formal charges were being filed against her, she must have felt as though a second assault had been made on her.

Somehow, Alana resolved, she had to find the courage to help Leslie Faye through this trial. The tools of her trade—research and observation—could make a substantial difference in the final outcome. She'd help Sylas Kincaid pick unbiased jurors. Leslie Faye would be found innocent of all charges. Then, yes then—a peculiar smile raised the corner of her mouth—she'd make certain Leslie Faye filed counter-charges against the bastard who'd perpetrated the crime. He'd be the one sent to jail.

Her tongue flicked across the roof of her mouth. The taste of poetic justice worked like an antacid to settle her stomach.

She scanned the baggage area while she stooped to pick up the strap of one of her suitcases. Leslie Faye was hustling a protesting man in a maroon uniform toward her.

"Lady, I'm supposed to be checking in luggage, not carrying it out. You're going to get me fired!"

"You were standing out there twiddling your thumbs," Leslie Faye retorted. "This will only take a few minutes if you quit dragging your feet!"

Her insistence restored Alana's ability to smile. She started wheeling her suitcases toward them.

"Give this kind gentleman your suitcases, Alana. He's generously offered to be useful." Blue eyes snapping a silent command, Leslie Faye stressed the last word.

"Lady, I told you. That's not my job!"

"We can manage without him," Alana interjected. "I'm feeling better."

The man in uniform bobbed his head, jerked his arm free from the small woman's fingers and rushed off in the opposite direction toward his assigned post.

Leslie Faye's eyes shot daggers at his retreating back. "What happened to the good old days when men were vying to carry a woman's luggage?"

"With the energy you used dragging him over here he probably thought you were capable of throwing the luggage out to the car," Alana teased. "C'mon, Mighty Mouse, let's get out of here."

Giggling at the nickname Alana had given her when she'd announced her intentions to sign up for the weight lifting class back in high school, Leslie Faye took one of the luggage straps.

Outside, she glanced at the threatening clouds hanging low in the sky. "Sometimes I wish I was still Mighty Mouse and you were still Bones. I'd even be willing to take the punishment for burying your mother's jewelry."

Alana grinned. "Grounded for life, remember?"

"Yeah. I hated being confined to my room."

An uneasy silence fell between them. They'd been friends too long not to know what the other was thinking. Confinement in a jail cell would be far worse than being restricted to a room filled with toys.

"I won't let them lock you up," Alana promised. She shifted her shoulder bag to the same arm that trailed her suitcase, then she draped the other arm across Leslie Faye's shoulders.

In return, Leslie Faye wrapped her free arm around her friend's waist. "I know you won't."

"It's a sad commentary on our justice system when a lunatic can drag a woman into a dark alley, attempt to violate her body and then go scot-free, while the woman is taken to the police station to be booked for assault and battery. That is what happened, isn't it?"

Without answering, Leslie Faye stopped beside a fire-engine-red convertible. She attempted to heave the suitcase over the side of the car and into the back seat.

Alana attributed her frown and clenched jaw to the size and weight of the piece of luggage. "Here. I'll get that," she said.

Leslie Faye stepped aside, opened her purse and began rummaging in it for her car keys.

Used to taking care of her own luggage, Alana quickly stowed both pieces in the back seat. She squeezed the passenger door handle, but it didn't open.

The top is down and the door is locked? she mused. A tremor shook her hand as she recalled the bizarre things she'd done after her own traumatic experience: milk in the cabinet, empty glass in the refrigerator; the stench of a pot burning on the stove; her wallet left at the grocery store. There were days she'd felt certain she had lost her mind.

"That isn't what happened," Leslie Faye said. She dangled her keys and sunglasses in front of her eyes as though she couldn't believe she'd found them. She unlocked both doors and scooted inside. "Ed Morgan is a slimeball, but he isn't a lunatic. I'd been out with him a couple of times before this happened."

Alana looked down at her hands. Mentally she willed them not to divulge her inner turmoil. She'd known Tom Lane, too. The roar in her ears grew louder than the sound of the engine roaring to life. She barely felt the car lurching backward, then accelerating forward. She entirely missed the stop at the gate to pay the parking fee.

Once they were on the highway headed south, Leslie Faye said, "Everybody likes him."

Everybody thought Tom was the best catch on campus.

"He owns a successful business."

Quarterback on the varsity football team.

"I met him at a chamber of commerce meeting. He was the guest speaker."

I met him at the library. He was working on a physics paper.

"You know how tongue-tied I get when I'm speaking to a crowd of strangers."

I couldn't pass chemistry, much less take a physics class.

"While I listened to him speak, I felt drawn to his good looks, his sense of humor, his cleverness."

Ditto!

Alana squirmed in her seat. The urge to put her hands over her ears to keep from hearing Leslie Faye's monologue and her own silent response was becoming compulsive.

She darted a quick glance at her friend. A casual observer would have seen merely a woman intent on her driving, on reaching her destination.

But Alana was a trained observer. She noticed Leslie Faye's jaw tighten, then relax as though she was making a conscious effort to continue reciting the painful events. Sunglasses concealed her eyes, but they couldn't hold back a tear sliding beneath them. Her knuckles appeared almost snow-white as she gripped the steering wheel.

Alana wanted to reach out and touch her. She wanted to stop her, to tell her she need not go on. The men and the places they met them were different, but their stories were painfully similar.

She had to admire Leslie Faye for having the guts to confide in her.

"The night...it...happened, he'd brought me a dozen carnations and taken me to dinner. He said he'd forgotten some papers that he needed to drop off at his office and asked if I'd mind stopping at his house. At the time I thought that was a little peculiar, but I ignored the tiny warning signal. What the hell, I'll admit it to you. I was curious about where he lived. I marched up the steps to his condo like a lamb being led to the slaughter—totally oblivious to the danger."

She swiped at the tears with the back of her hand. "Damn, I hate crying. Half the time I don't realize I'm doing it."

Alana nodded sympathetically. She couldn't speak. Silent tears were trickling down her throat.

"Anyway, we went into his condo. He offered me a glass of white wine, which I accepted. Like a dumb-bell, I sat down on the sofa. While he poured us a drink, I remember thinking, 'He was so anxious to get those papers to his office. Why hasn't he gotten them?' He handed me the wine.... And the next thing I knew I heard his pants hit the floor! I felt like a complete ignoramus. I started to get up. I made some smart-aleck comment about his boxer shorts, thinking that would cool his ardor. It d-didn't. He p-pushed me flat on the sofa. I told him I wasn't interested in him s-sexually.''

"I get the picture," Alana groaned through tightly compressed lips. Leslie Faye's stammer more than her tears warned Alana that she had gone about as far as she could go without breaking down completely. "He made advances and you hit him with something."

"No, Alana, don't stop me. I have to t-tell you everything." She cleared her throat loudly. "Yeah, I hit him on the side of the head with a stone sculpture of a fish that was on the coffee table. He rolled to the carpet, screaming and shouting at me, calling me filthy names. By then, I'd seen the blood running down his face. I was hysterical. I was screaming, too."

She inhaled deeply. "His neighbors called the police. They arrived, sirens blaring. Ed knew one of the officers. God, it was like old-home week. From there on, it's a blur in my mind. I couldn't believe this was happening to me. I remember the handcuffs. And I remember hearing something about Ed going to the hospital to get stitches. I must have blocked out the ride to the police station. I did have sense enough to call Gregory. He's the one who got me out of there."

Alana hesitated. She had to ask questions, questions that were important to how the case would be handled in court. The fact that she was mired in memories of her own trauma made the chore difficult.

"Did he physically hurt you?" Her voice was hoarse.

"No."

"Did he verbally threaten you?"

"Yes. Violent threats." Leslie Faye raked the back of her hand beneath her nose. She removed her sunglasses. Dark smudges of brown mascara ringed her eyes. "Get me a tissue out of the console, will you?"

Alana considered offering to drive, but she knew she wasn't in any shape to get behind the wheel of a car she wasn't used to when it took three attempts for her to unlatch the lid of the center console.

She plucked three tissues from the box, two for Leslie Faye and one for herself.

The lid fell back into place automatically. Alana stared at it. She had to slam the door on her memories. She was twenty-nine now—a savvy career woman, not a naive, trusting nineteen-year-old. She paid heed now to silent alarms Leslie Faye had ignored. Never again would a man get Alana in a compromising situation!

Leslie Faye took the tissues dangling from Alana's fingers. She blew her nose on one, then wiped her eyes with the other. She glanced at her reflection in the rearview mirror and groaned, "I'm a mess. Red nose. Raccoon eyes. Gregory hates it when I blubber."

"Do you want to stop at a gas station to freshen your makeup?"

"No. They'll be waiting for us. Gregory's been a big help to me since this happened." She glanced furtively at Alana. "We've been sort of dating. I guess that's what it's called even though we're divorced."

When she didn't get any reaction from Alana over that bombshell, she returned her eyes to he road. "I don't want to keep him waiting. You know how he is when I'm ten seconds late."

Alana nodded. When she was Leslie Faye's roommate in college, Gregory's being habitually late had irked Alana; he believed that losing track of time while he studied at the law library was a valid excuse. But if Leslie Faye was tardy because she was studying Gregory would sulk the entire evening.

Hard feelings between Gregory and Alana had stemmed from her constantly defending Leslie Faye. By the end of their freshman year, she seldom double-dated with her roomie because the evening usually ended with Alana biting her tongue to keep from giving Gregory the tongue-lashing he deserved.

Gregory Hale was at the bottom of her list of favorite people. Silently she thanked her lucky stars that she'd be working with Gregory's partner, Sylas Kincaid.

"Is Mr. Kincaid anything like Gregory?" Self-centered, overambitious, Alana silently tacked on.

"Gregory says he's extremely competent, if that's what you mean." Leslie Faye wadded the tissues and tucked them in her purse. She shot Alana a watery grin and bumped her elbow. "Good-looking, too. He was the best man at my wedding. You'd have been his date if you'd been able to be there. He's single. Six feet two inches, dark hair, fabulous gray eyes."

"Stop it."

"What?" Leslie Faye asked, feigning innocence.

"Matchmaking."

"Matchmaking? That's not a bad idea. I've often thought the two of you . . ."

"Don't bother."

Leslie Faye's mercurial temperament allowed her to switch from her personal disaster to matchmaking with the same agility she showed steering the car off the Gulf Freeway. Alana had to change the direction of her friend's thoughts, or in one giant leap she'd go from Kincaid as the best man at her wedding to him as the groom at Alana's wedding!

"It's no bother. It would be my pleasure."

"Leslie Faye—"

"If the two of you fell in love, you could move back to Galveston and it would be like old times for us."

"Leslie Faye—"

"You and Sylas could double with Gregory and me. We could go sailing on Greg's boat or rock hop fishing at the jetties and have picnics and..."

"Leslie Faye, stop it!" Alana's hand sliced the air in a cut-it-off motion. Those were adolescent dreams she'd had before Tom Lane trapped her in his dorm room. Neither she nor Leslie Faye would ever be the same again. Didn't Leslie Faye realize that? "I'm here to help you. I am not here husband hunting. Do you understand?"

"No, I don't," Leslie Faye replied stubbornly. She gave Alana a peculiar look. "You don't have a significant other, do you?"

"No. With my job I'm never in one place long enough to start a relationship."

"Then what's wrong with my matchmaking?" Leslie Faye persisted. "Don't you think it's time you came home and settled down?"

Alana's patience had been stretched to its limit. "No, I don't think it's time for me to get married and have two point six children! End of discussion."

"Why can't we discuss this like two rational adults?"

"Because we've quarreled about marriage versus career a million times, before we graduated from high school. You wanted to get married and have two point six children, and I wanted a career. Okay, so you got married and I have an extremely satisfying career. I'm happy with my choice. I don't want to hear you humming the wedding march when you introduce me to Sylas Kincaid. Let it be. Please."

Leslie Faye made a right turn at Seawall Boulevard and goosed the gas peddle. "Are you implying that since I divorced Gregory and opened the accessory shop, you must have won that argument?"

"I'm implying nothing of the kind." Alana inhaled a deep breath of salty air. She had to grin as she said, "Do you realize I've been here less than an hour and we're fighting exactly like we used to over the very same things?"

"Yeah." Leslie Faye returned her smile. "It feels good. We always did fight like cats and dogs, but heaven help anyone who said anything against one of us to the other. I guess it's kind of normal for the two of us, huh?"

"I guess so." Alana reached across the console between the seats and squeezed her friend's hand. She felt the pressure returned. "Do you think we'll ever outgrow bickering with each other?"

"I can't think of anyone I'd rather fight with . . . or have in my corner of the boxing ring when the bell rings."

"Ditto."

Sharp pangs of guilt and shame stabbed Alana. Guilt for having curtailed their friendship and for having been unable to share her problem with Leslie Faye. Shame for having trusted a man and having gotten herself into such a stupid predicament.

"Alana? You're looking a little green around the gills again. Should I pull over? Are you going to be sick?"

"No. Honestly, I'm fine." Keep telling yourself that, she coached. One day it will be true.

Chapter Three

Six foot two, dark hair, fabulous gray eyes, Alana mused. Her friend's description of Sylas Kincaid had understated the man's physical assets. His wide shoulders, muscular chest and powerful shoulders dwarfed Gregory's slender build.

Her silent alarm system bleeped as her eyes swept over Leslie Faye's lawyer.

Responsive to the alert, she focused on Gregory Hale instead. The years had been kind to him. He still looked as though he'd just been elected president of the student council.

Except for his hands, she decided. One of them was rumpling his light brown hair, while the other was fidgeting with the front button of his suit jacket.

He'd always been uneasy around her.

The feeling was mutual, Alana thought. He'd been a hotshot fraternity man, a candidate for a student body election whom she had suspected of carrying an absentee ballot tucked in his back pocket, one for her to mark in case she hadn't voted for him. And he'd always known how she'd vote if he handed it to her.

Alana transferred her gaze back to Sylas Kincaid as she tolerated an unenthusiastic hug from Gregory.

Kincaid must have belonged to a different fraternity than Gregory. Or more than likely, he hadn't belonged to one at all. He had the rugged looks of an independent man who didn't care who voted for or against him.

She noticed him studying her with slow deliberation. Dark eyelashes combined with his mahogany tan to create a striking contrast. He had the sort of eyes a woman would never forget.

Definitely a man to be wary of, she concluded, listening to the danger signals coming from the dark corners of her mind.

"Alana, this is Sylas Kincaid," Leslie Faye said. "Sylas, Alana Benton."

His assessing gray eyes met her slightly defiant brown ones and held them with confidence. Alana understood then why Leslie Faye trusted him. He had the penetrating stare of a man a woman could count on, regardless of how dirty the opponents wanted to fight.

As though on cue, he extended his hand as she raised hers. A man's handshake gave Alana insights into his attitudes toward women. If he clasped only her fingers in a courtly manner and raked his thumb over the back of her hand, the handshake had sexual connotations. If he clenched her hand in a knuckle-busting grip, the handshake was proof that he considered himself physically dominant.

Kincaid's grip, thumb to thumb, palm to palm, his fingers curling around the heel of her hand and exerting a firm, steady pressure, indicated he considered her an equal.

"Welcome back to Texas," he greeted her before turning her hand loose. "Leslie Faye and Gregory have spoken of you often."

Attuned to everything going on around her, she noticed Gregory had pulled Leslie Faye aside. She heard him mumble, "You've been crying. She upset you, didn't she?"

"Mixed reviews?" Alana asked Sylas bluntly. Her eyebrow arched, demanding a candid reply.

"Rave reviews, from both of them."

His choice of words amused Alana. Rave, as in rant and rave, would have been Gregory's review; rave, as in praise, was how Leslie Faye would have spoken of her. Kincaid had refrained from the usual polite lie in favor of double entendre.

A slow smile curved her mouth. Softly, so as not to be overheard, she said, "Don't believe everything you've heard, from either Gregory or Leslie Faye. Neither of them is unbiased."

Abruptly, she wheeled around, in time to deflect the heated glare Gregory shot at her back. Her teeth clenched as she glanced at Leslie Faye, who clung limply to Gregory's arm. In less than five minutes, Gregory had taken the steel out of Leslie Faye's backbone.

Who was he to criticize Alana for being responsible for his ex-wife's tears? Undoubtedly her friend had shed buckets of tears over him, before she worked up the courage to divorce him. If he'd taken care of his marriage with the same diligence he expended on his law practice, Leslie Faye wouldn't have been in this predicament. She wouldn't have been dating another man. Where was Gregory the night Leslie Faye went to Ed Morgan's apartment?

To Alana's way of thinking, Gregory had no grounds to be critical of her.

"Can I get your suitcases from the car?" Sylas asked, in an obvious attempt to defuse the explosive anger that was coursing between Alana and his law partner.

It was on the tip of Alana's tongue to refuse Kincaid's offer, but she bit back the impulse. She had to get Gregory out of sight or she'd give him the tongue-lashing he richly deserved.

"Thank you," she replied, forcing a genial smile. "I'll go with you."

From the courtyard where they'd met the men, Alana marched toward the car, which Leslie Faye had parked in the ground-level garage beneath the elevated condominiums.

"These condos hadn't been built the last time you were here, had they?" Sylas asked, matching Alana's stride on the narrow sidewalk.

"No."

Unintentionally his jacket sleeve brushed against her forearm. Although her mind remained on what she'd have liked to tell Gregory Hale, she automatically widened the space between herself and the man beside her.

Before she started working on Leslie Faye's case, she planned on having a heart-to-heart chat with Gregory. She had to sort through what she'd like to tell him, and what she would tell him.

She positively would not let him undermine her friend's confidence in herself. The jurors would be sympathetic to Leslie Faye because of her size and appearance, but they'd take her for a complete phony if they thought she was trying to project the image of a submissive woman who'd allow a man to dominate her. Leslie Faye had to show that despite her size, she was spunky. And if Leslie Faye continued to wilt in Gregory's presence, Alana would bar him from her courtroom.

Sylas pretended to ignore her curt reply. "A few years back a rumor spread through the community that the Texas legislature was going to legalize gambling on Galveston Island. Condos, apartments and hotels sprouted up like Texas bluebonnets in the hill country."

"Oh?" Alana replied, totally distracted by her inner turmoil.

She would inform Gregory that she didn't give a damn whether he approved of her being on this case. He wasn't the one on trial. She didn't need his permission. Leslie Faye wanted her here. Period.

If she brought up her fee, which she felt certain he would, she'd politely—no, pointedly—remind him that he no longer had a voice in the spending of his wife's trust fund—not that Alana planned on charging her friend for her services.

"Watch out for that dragon snapping at your heels."

Reflexively, she stopped and looked down, then back over her shoulder. Sylas stood beside Leslie Faye's convertible, several cars behind her. "What'd you say?"

"You were obviously slaying imaginary demons from hell," Sylas teased, grinning at her. He lifted her suitcases from the back seat of the car. Her go-to-hell-Gregory Hale attitude intrigued him. "I thought I'd guard your flank for you."

"Hell spelled H-a-l-e?" she countered, imitating his soft Texas drawl as she transposed his word as easily as he'd twisted the meaning of the word *rave*.

"They do sound alike, don't they?" Sylas admired quick-witted women. "Tell me, were you winning or losing the battle?"

"Eventually, I always win," she replied, matching his brand of self-confidence with pure audacity. "How about you?"

Sylas chuckled. He also liked a woman who knew her own worth. "Something tells me you've switched from mind battles to court battles. Right?"

She hadn't, but with a nod of her head she admitted to being curious about his win-loss record. "I suspect you seldom lose in the courtroom, Mr. Kincaid."

"I win my fair share."

I'll bet you do, she mused, following him to the back of the garage where an enclosed staircase led upward. She noticed he hadn't bothered to make use of the wheels on the suitcases. He carried them with little effort.

Mindful of his manners, he waited for Alana to precede him up the steps.

Out of habit, she glanced upward, then scanned the parking lot before saying, "Lead the way. You know where you're going."

"Second floor. Third door on the left. Number twenty-six."

Acutely aware of where the level of his eyes would be when she mounted the steps, she made certain her hips barely swayed. She also made a conscious effort to forget the man behind her and to concentrate on the upcoming confrontation with Gregory.

She'd made one scene at the airport; she wasn't certain she was up to another.

The smell of rain grew stronger with each rising step. Alana knew the storm would begin within minutes. Unless she governed her temper, that storm would rage both inside and outside Leslie Faye's condo.

They were on the second floor landing when Sylas moved beside her and said, "I've been requested to tell you that your expertise isn't needed on this case."

Alana shot Kincaid a sidelong glance. The look of distaste on his face told her that Gregory's partner felt obligated to inform her of Gregory's opinion, but didn't necessarily agree with it. In fact, when she looked down at the grip he had on her suitcase, she intuitively knew he'd argue with her if she simply agreed.

To test her theory, she replied, "Perhaps it isn't."

The corners of his mouth tilted downward.

"But then again," she added, "I don't really give a damn what Gregory requested, nor will I abide by his decision. He isn't the one up for assault and battery...yet."

Sylas's lips widened into a smile. He stopped outside the door, dropping one suitcase. This close, he could see haunting shadows in Alana's dark eyes. Had hearing Gregory's request caused her pain? he wondered. But he didn't think so.

Alana stepped back, consciously widening the circle of privacy around herself. Her eyes dropped to the Windsor knot of Sylas's tie. Her hand reached for the doorknob.

His hand closing over hers detained her. She schooled her face to an expressionless mask. She slid her hand from beneath his as though unwilling to make an issue over who opened the door.

"For friendship's sake I had to honor Gregory's request, but for the record I want you to know that I'm not always in agreement with him," Sylas said.

She took a step sideways, feeling the cedar board siding snag her linen jacket. He braced the flat of his hand to the right of her head, silently demanding that she stop her retreat. Her heart began hammering in her chest. The humid air, dense with moisture, became difficult to breathe. She had to get away from him.

She reacted as any snared animal would behave. She curled her lip and snarled. "Bully for you."

His jaw jerked as though she'd slapped him. His arm dropped to his side. Before he could recover his composure, she'd opened the door and disappeared inside the condo.

Instantly, Alana regretted her spontaneous response. This case would be difficult at best. The last thing she needed to do was to antagonize Leslie Faye's lawyer. She exhaled the air trapped in her lungs, disturbing the fringe of bangs on her brow.

So far this had been one hell of a day, from the minute she'd picked up the phone and heard Leslie Faye's voice. She'd made a spectacle of herself at the airport, relived her nightmare, quarreled with her friend and insulted the man she had to work with. And she still had to deal with Gregory, when all she wanted to do was crawl in bed and pull the covers over her head.

Voices coming from the living room—Gregory's intent, Leslie Faye's weepy—brought Alana out of her moment of self-pity. She crossed to the doorway.

Leslie Faye was curled up in the corner of the sofa with a pillow clutched to her chest, and Gregory, standing at the window with his hands on his hips and back to the room, was giving her friend what for.

"She had the gall to interrogate you about what happened while you were driving home?" Gregory asked, plowing his fingers through his hair. "That bitch! She didn't have to put you through the wringer. I could have answered her questions."

Alana stepped forward as she heard Kincaid enter the kitchen behind her. "Hearsay evidence is unacceptable in a court of law, Gregory, just in case you planned on taking the witness stand on Leslie Faye's behalf."

Leslie Faye pushed the pillow aside and jumped to her feet. "How about my fixing all of us something to drink? A pitcher of golden margaritas?"

"Make mine a Wild Turkey, on the rocks," Gregory said. Giving Alana a cold smirk, he added, "You'd better make it black coffee for her."

Leslie Faye blushed to the roots of her blond curls and hurried into the kitchen.

Alana focused her eyes on the Gulf's whitecaps to keep them from rolling heavenward. Did Leslie Faye have to tell him about Alana's "delayed airsickness"? He had plenty of reasons to dislike her without adding lush to the list.

"A Coke would do nicely," she said, purposely contradicting him. "Can I help?"

"No. You make yourself at home. You've had a long trip."

Before Leslie Faye vanished into the kitchen, Alana saw the give-her-a-break-she's-my-guest look she gave Gregory. He shrugged, then impaled Alana with his blue eyes. Coming farther into the living room, she didn't so much as blink under his careful scrutiny.

"Where do you want these?" Sylas asked Leslie Faye as he held up Alana's suitcases.

"In the guest bedroom. Down the hall, first door on the right. The usual for you?"

"Yeah. Thanks."

Sylas took one look at the pair in the living room and shivered. He'd need a blowtorch to get through the frigid air ringing the two of them. He strode down the hallway eager to get back before they started taking verbal potshots at each other.

Primly seated on the edge of the sofa cushion, legs crossed demurely at the ankles, her skirt hem pulled well below her knees, Alana felt capable of dealing with any additional names Gregory dared to call her.

No one, absolutely no one, called her a bitch and got away with it! Not since Tom Lane!

"Here we are," Leslie Faye said, putting a glass filled with ice and a small bottle of Coke on the end table beside Alana.

"Thanks." Had they been alone, she'd have commented on Leslie Faye's having taken the trouble to find a store that still stocked Cokes in six-ounce bottles. Leslie Faye had often used to tease her about being the only Coca-Cola connoisseur in the state of Texas.

Leslie Faye crossed to the love seat where Gregory sat. "Bourbon for you and a cold beer for Sylas." She put the beer on the glass-topped coffee table. "How about some fresh shrimp, right off the boat? With that special hot sauce you like, Gregory."

He nodded, without looking at her. "Sylas, come on in here and we'll plan our strategy while she's fixing the shrimp."

"Don't you think Leslie Faye should be a part of this?" *Since it directly involves her?* Alana silently completed the question. She didn't want Gregory's hostility to flow into her work.

"You go ahead, honey," Gregory said to Leslie Faye. "I'll brief you later on what we discuss."

Alana sipped her Coke, hoping the beverage would wash down her objections. How Leslie Faye could duke it out toe-to-toe with her, and an hour later docilely roll over and play dead for Gregory, was beyond Alana's comprehension.

After Leslie Faye had left the room and Sylas had taken a seat on the other end of the sofa where Alana sat, Gregory added, "She knows I have her best interests at heart."

I won't let him provoke me, Alana told herself, dropping her eyes to the end table where she placed her drink. Speak to him as though he's Joe Doe from Kokomo. Taking care of the business at hand didn't allow room for personal animosities.

In a civil tone, she asked, "What line of defense do you plan to use?"

"Self-defense," Sylas answered. "Ed Morgan accosted Leslie Faye. She defended herself."

"We feel Leslie Faye's size and demeanor will justify her using a stone ornament," Gregory said. "Ed is twice her size."

Sylas leaned toward her. "I've checked the computer for similar cases. They're few and far between. I assume in a case where a woman injures a man he isn't prone to getting the police involved. The few cases like this that were brought to judicial hearings were those rare ones where a wife abused her husband."

Gregory sniggered. "No *real* man wants it to be a matter of public record that he can't handle his wife."

Alana adopted a bland expression to hide her reaction to Gregory's remark. "We don't have much statistical information to go on as far as the jurors' attitudes, do we?"

"No," Sylas answered. "I've had a devil of a time finding any written materials on the subject. I did find a few magazine articles, a couple of books, and I've seen a couple of talk shows on matters of this nature, but I don't know how the average person would interpret what happened."

"It's standard operation in my line of work to conduct what I call a man-on-the-street survey." Alana paused, waiting for a reaction. When Sylas nodded his head, she continued. "Would it be possible for me to go over your research material?"

"Haven't you ever handled a case like this?" Gregory asked, obviously appalled by her lack of experience.

Before she could answer, Sylas said, "*I* haven't. Is that a problem?"

"Of course not. My asking you to handle this case was a vote of confidence in you." Gregory glanced from Sylas to Alana. "I just thought that since Alana is an expert, she'd be familiar with this sort of thing."

Alana ignored Gregory's condescending remark. "Leslie Faye mentioned she met Mr. Morgan when he was a guest speaker at a chamber of commerce meeting. What else do we know about him?"

"Other than that he's in business for himself, not much," Sylas replied.

"Police record?"

"I checked that out. He's clean," Gregory answered.

"What about his personal life?" She directed her inquiry to Sylas. He shook his head. "We need to know if this is a typical pattern for him. I'd suggest hiring a private investigator."

"What a waste of money!" Gregory raised his eyes toward the ceiling as though she'd made a totally asinine suggestion. "Ed Morgan doesn't have *stupid* written on his forehead. Do you honestly think he'd pull this kind of stunt again? Before the trial?"

"I don't know whether he would or wouldn't. But I'd be interested in knowing who he's presently dating and who he's dated in the past. If we can find a witness who is willing to testify that Ed Morgan tried to rape her, then—"

"Rape?" Gregory barked, rising to his feet. "Who said anything about rape?"

Surprised, wondering if she'd missed out on something, Alana looked up at him and replied, "Leslie Faye told me she hit him because he attempted to—"

"You listen to me, Alana Benton." Gregory shook his finger in her face. "I don't want my wife held up to ridicule in this community. Rape is a four letter word around here."

"Wait a minute. I'm confused." She couldn't believe that Leslie Faye's protecting her virtue would not be the kingpin of the case. Alana had all she could do to keep from slapping her forehead in frustration. She turned toward Sylas and asked softly, "Are you telling me that you're going into court to defend Leslie Faye, treating this as though the two of them were arguing and she hit him?"

Sylas rose. He looked Gregory straight in the eye as he answered her. "We discussed that possibility, but I feel it would be a weak defense."

"I won't allow you or anybody else to drag her name through the muck. I'm telling you, there isn't a jury in Texas who'd convict Leslie Faye. This trial is just a formality. In the heat of anger, Morgan pressed charges. The prosecuting attorney took the case because he's made a big deal out of this law-and-order thing." Gregory pointed at Sylas, then back at himself. "You know, and I know that if Ed Morgan has a lick of sense—which he does—he'll drop the charges and this will never go to court!"

At that inopportune moment, the subject of their heated discussion entered the room carrying a silver tray piled high with steamed shrimp. "Time to take a break?"

Alana edged backward into the corner of the couch. Gregory glared at Sylas. Leslie Faye scooted between the two men.

"Alana, this hot sauce is for Gregory," she warned, pointing to the crystal bowl at the right of the tray. "Don't try it or you'll think your tongue's caught on fire. I'll be right back with something tame for the rest of us."

She breezed out of the room and was back in less than two seconds with another bowl of sauce and a stack of plates. Grinning, she waited until Gregory and

Sylas had returned to their seats before asking, "How's the war council going?"

"Don't you worry about it, sweetheart. I'll take care of everything," Gregory replied. He patted the cushion of the love seat beside him. "Sit down and we'll dig into those shrimp. They look great, huh, Sylas?"

Alana noticed Sylas rubbing the back of his neck. Reading his body language brightened her outlook. Maybe she wasn't the only one in the room who thought Gregory Hale was a pain in the neck.

"What?" Sylas asked. His thoughts had been directed toward finding some middle ground on which to build the case.

"I said the shrimp look great," Gregory repeated. "Dig in."

Alana chose to freshen her Coke while the others bent over the platter. Unable to believe she'd missed vital clues that would have indicated earlier the line of defense, she replayed the discussion in her mind.

She'd missed conspicuous signs. Neither Sylas nor Gregory had called this an attempted rape case. She'd heard words and phrases such as "accosted," "in cases like this," "matters of this nature" and "self-defense." She should have picked up on the omission of one vital word.

Why hadn't she?

She could make excuses for the oversight, but one valid reason bothered her. Gregory and Sylas weren't the only ones in the room having difficulty dealing with Leslie Faye's trauma.

Stop it! She ordered herself. She was guilty of using nice phrases to conceal the ugly truth, too. Rape. R-a-p-e. She had to deal with it or she'd be useless in the courtroom. If she had to go back to elementary

school learning techniques and write the word five
hundred times before she felt comfortable using it, she
would.

Slowly she stirred the ice cubes in her glass with the
tip of her finger. She wondered if Kincaid's research
revolved around a woman assaulting a man or around
date rape. She raised her eyes, looking at him through
a fringe of dark lashes.

What kind of a man was he? He'd relayed Gregory's message that she wouldn't be needed on the case,
but on the other hand, he'd openly disagreed with
him, in front of her. What sort of a tightrope was he
walking? On one side, he was Gregory's friend and
law partner. And on the other side was presumably his
desire to defend Leslie Faye to the best of his ability.

Could she trust him to put his work over his friendship? Was he a dedicated professional or one of the
good-ol'-boy attorneys who expected everybody and
everything to fall in line behind him?

Alana had little faith in her good judgment when it
came to personal relationships with men, but she
considered her professional judgment sound. Her initial reaction had been that Sylas Kincaid was a man
Leslie Faye would want in her corner.

Her lips tightened into a thin line. She could only
hope her return to Texas hadn't fouled up her intuition. One thing for certain, it wasn't going to take long
to find out. Once Gregory was out of earshot she'd
have that question answered PDQ.

First thing in the morning she'd be in Kincaid's office asking pertinent questions. Gregory's hope that
Ed Morgan would drop the charges wouldn't stop her
from making sure Leslie Faye's attorney was prepared to go to court.

The bottom line, she resolved, was the jurors would find Leslie Faye innocent of all charges. Then would come the next step.

Alana put down her drink, picked up a plate and chose several shrimp.

"Try some of my hot sauce," Gregory offered, a smirk on his face.

"No, thanks." So help me, she thought, if he tells me it'll grow hair on my chest, he'll have reason to have *me* booked for assault and battery!

"So," Leslie Faye said, "tell us about living in St. Louis. Aren't the winters frightful?"

"Last winter I was in sunny California working on a civil liberties case." She nibbled on a shrimp, hoping the subject would be directed away from her.

"Oh, yeah." Leslie Faye picked up the social ball again. "The letter in your Christmas card mentioned that. Something to do with union problems, wasn't it?"

"Um-hmm." Alana's answer was not meant to intrigue the listeners, merely to beg off discussing the case by refusing to talk with her mouth full.

Gregory dunked a shrimp in his red sauce and looked at Sylas. "Remember that insurance case against the railroad company that I was handling? Now, that was a tough one."

Sylas pretended to be listening to Gregory's recounting of the case, but his attention was focused on Alana.

Quick-witted and independent. And from the incident on the balcony, he'd concluded she wasn't a woman to be intimidated when she felt backed into a corner.

Alana Benton was a fighter.

Tough on the outside, and yet he had the gut-level feeling she was vulnerable, too. He'd noticed how she distanced herself from him on the sidewalk. When he inadvertently covered her hand on the doorknob, she'd flinched.

Did she think he was making a pass at her?

Quickly, he took another sidelong glance. From Gregory's meager description, he'd formed a mental image of the Wicked Witch of the West. The reality was somewhere between the beauty queen Leslie had raved about and the magazine photograph he'd seen in *Significant People*, he decided.

When she glanced in his direction, he centered his attention on the beer bottle in his hand.

Physical features were a biological blessing or curse, as the case might be. In Alana's particular case, she'd been blessed. But Sylas knew from previous experiences with women that good looks could often be superficial. What attracted him to a particular woman was what went on in her head, and when he got to know her, what went on in her heart.

He'd only just met Alana. He felt a natural curiosity about those soulful dark eyes of hers, but he didn't know her well enough to make a pass.

So why was she so damned defensive?

If she'd come into his office and asked him to handle her divorce, he'd have wagered hard cold cash that she'd been the scapegoat for a man with heavy fists. There had to be a reason for the imaginary barbed wire fence she'd posted around herself. But from what Leslie Faye had said, Alana wasn't married and never had been.

His interest piqued, he turned toward Alana. She raised her head until their eyes met.

What are you hiding, Alana? he silently asked.

The puzzled frown wrinkling his brow made his thoughts easily discernible to Alana. He was wondering about her, about how she would fit into his upcoming court case. Alana hesitated, then smiled congenially. It was her way of apologizing for what had happened at the back door.

"Our client didn't lose one red cent in damages, did they, Sylas?"

Sylas caught the dirty look his partner flung in his direction. Gregory had apparently misconstrued Sylas's open stare and Alana's smile as a betrayal of their partnership.

"You won the case, but I'd wager the company's victory lights were dimmed when they received their bill," Sylas replied facetiously.

"A tax write-off," Gregory scoffed, picking up the platter and striding toward the kitchen. He motioned for Leslie Faye to join him. "Even Uncle Sam knows you can't get something for nothing. Ed Morgan is going to learn that lesson, too. He'll be making a laughingstock out of himself, you wait and see."

Alana waited until Gregory couldn't overhear her, then asked Sylas, "So, do you think the essence of Ed Morgan's case is that he tried to get something for nothing and failed?"

"I'm certain Morgan's male ego has been punctured, but according to written law that isn't a criminal offense." Sylas deliberately rolled his tongue in his cheek, choosing to minimize the seriousness of Leslie Faye's striking Ed Morgan until he and Alana were at his office discussing the merits of the case. "I'd estimate half the female population would be locked up and the other half would be on trial if the police arrested women for wielding ego deflators. Wouldn't you agree?"

"I'll plead the Fifth Amendment," she replied dryly.

His warm chuckle and lopsided grin made her alarm system jangle. Warily, she straightened her relaxed pose and relied on a tried-and-true method of lowering the voltage of a man's kilowatt smile.

She yawned.

His smile grew broader. "That'll get you eight to ten."

Some men simply couldn't take a subtle hint. "Sorry. It's been a long day, all things considered."

"Do you read in bed?" he asked. His gray eyes sparked with pure devilry.

"I beg your pardon?"

"I said—"

"I heard what you said, Mr. Kincaid, but I don't discuss my bedroom habits with strangers." Put that in your beer bottle, shake it up, remove your thumb and see if it dampens your charisma!

He almost preferred to see her eyes snapping angrily at him than to see in them the flickering shadows his teasing had caused. Almost, but not quite.

"I left some books here for Leslie Faye to read." He pushed back the cuff of his suit jacket to glance at his watch. "You might find them . . . of interest."

Her imagination kicked into high gear. Was he twisting the word *interest* until it had a double meaning? "One of those tawdry spy thrillers Leslie Faye loves?"

"No. You don't strike me as a woman who needs to get her thrills vicariously. Your job provides the excitement in your life, doesn't it?"

Lazily he stood, then offered his hand to assist her from the sofa's plush cushions. He felt like a beggar who'd had a penny instead of the hoped-for quarter dropped in his hand when Alana gracefully rose without touching his hand.

"Absolutely," she confirmed. "Passion for one's work is far more satisfying than spy thrillers."

She turned toward the hallway to avoid letting him see the cost of her cavalier remark. Her face burned with chagrin. She knew she sounded like a pompous ass, but she seemed to have lost control over her mouth.

He refused to stop her progress until she reached the credenza where Leslie Faye had put the books he'd given her.

"In that case, you won't be combining business with pleasure. Business *is* your pleasure." In four long strides he closed the distance between them. He picked up one hardcover book and handed it to her, then strode toward the kitchen. "Sweet dreams, Alana."

Alana read the book's title, *Date Rape: Attitudes in Conflict*, and wanted to hurl it at his broad shoulders. He'd purposely led her to believe he was Gregory's puppet!

She opened the text to the index, rapidly skimming the list of subjects, then quietly closed it and returned it to the pile of books. She couldn't help a grimace of distress and distaste.

The sound of Leslie Faye's giggle drew her eyes toward the kitchen. Sylas Kincaid was nonchalantly leaning against the doorjamb, watching Alana, a befuddled expression on his face.

After the clever line she'd tossed like a gauntlet at his feet, she couldn't explain her actions without revealing the truth. Merely reading the author's introduction to the text would cause her vivid nightmares. He'd have to put whatever connotation he chose on her refusal to begin research.

Frankly, she didn't give a damn what he thought. Self-preservation came first.

A sad smile curved her mouth as she walked down the hall to the guest bedroom. Frankly? she questioned. She had to do one of two things—stop lying to herself, or drop the cue word that signaled to her that she was about to tell a lie.

She entered the spare bedroom, closed the door and, out of habit, turned the button on the knob to lock it. Her eyes darted around the four corners of the room, then settled on the suitcase Kincaid had placed on her bed.

She could try closing her eyes and imagining herself in another city, in a hotel room, preparing to unpack and start a new case. Normally, the challenge of being directly involved in someone else's problems would keep her too busy to be worried about her past.

But Alana knew pretending she was elsewhere wouldn't work. This time, her usual routines wouldn't allay her fears. She had to keep her eyes open and face the facts.

She groaned inwardly and moved to the center of the room. Leslie Faye's case was too close to what had happened to her. Each psychological jab her friend felt had an impact on Alana.

Leslie Faye didn't need to verbalize her hopes and fears; Alana knew them. They were written on her own heart. She fully understood why her friend had called her. Alana heard her silent plea to make everything the way it used to be. Leslie Faye wanted everything in her life to return to normal. Alana was in touch with that emotion. After she transferred to Stephens College, she'd spent countless hours daydreaming about being at home, being safe and secure.

But her experience had one major difference from Leslie Faye's. The minute Leslie Faye was arrested, all of Galveston Island began speculating about what had happened. Alana had avoided that by keeping her mouth shut, finishing the semester and fleeing to Missouri.

As she unzipped her suitcase, she wondered which was the toughest—knowing everyone was talking about what had happened, but getting emotional support from friends, or fleeing to avoid the gossip, but having to deal with the problem alone.

Only time could answer that question.

In her case, she'd been able to function as a normal human being when she consciously made the decision not to think about what had happened. But she had to admit, the moment Leslie Faye told her Ed Morgan had attempted to rape her, Alana had fallen apart. Memories of that awful night had spilled from the recesses of her mind like a movie film being dropped from its canister. Mental pictures she'd buried flashed on the backs of her eyelids in living color.

She sincerely hoped that because Leslie Faye was being forced to talk about what had happened, she would talk it out of her system. Alana now knew that what she'd tucked away in the darkest corner of her mind was still there.

She sighed, shaking her head. Maybe working through her friend's problem would be some sort of therapy. Maybe she could talk to herself and get this out of her system.

Alana raised the lid of her suitcase and stared at the materials she'd brought to educate Kincaid on techniques for selecting an unbiased jury. Her eyes moved to the door, and mentally beyond the door to where his books remained on the credenza.

This time she'd be the one doing the learning.

"And I'm not certain I'm ready to investigate this subject," she whispered. She could feel tears pooling in her eyes. She blinked her eyelids to stem their flow and looked at the bright light overhead.

"Why me? Why Leslie Faye? This shouldn't have happened to either of us!"

Chapter Four

Alana read the address Leslie Faye had written on a scrap of paper, then glanced at the cluster of offices opposite the Seawall. This had to be the place. She parked the car she'd rented earlier and got out carrying the research materials she wanted Kincaid to start on. She'd have brought his books, also, but they had vanished from Leslie Faye's credenza.

The Gulf breeze whipped the hem of her navy-blue shirtwaist dress around her legs. As she began searching for the sign Leslie Faye had said would be hanging outside the offices of Hale and Kincaid, she couldn't help but turn her eyes toward the ocean.

The spring storm had abated during the wee hours of the morning. Blue sky and blue waters stretched as far as the eye could see. Across the six-lane street, vacationers with cameras strung around their necks strolled along the sidewalk. A few energetic Galvestonians, dressed in shorts and tops, jogged between the walkers.

Alana inhaled deeply. The balmy weather and the salt air seemed to restore her energy level. Sleep had been evasive during the night. Her mind had worked overtime on Leslie Faye's problem, but now, with the sun shining overhead, Alana felt as though she'd slept soundly.

She resisted the urge to dawdle. She'd made an appointment with Kincaid's secretary before she left the condo. Arriving late wouldn't improve the bad impression she'd made yesterday, she mused, as she hastened toward the strip of offices.

She tilted her head back and began reading the signs projecting from the building's front. Gulfcoast Insurance. Tracy's Gift Shop. Hale and Kincaid, Law Offices. She checked her watch and grinned. Two minutes early.

Reaching for the door handle, her eyes widened as a bell jingled and it opened.

"Good morning, Alana," Sylas said in greeting. "Beautiful day, huh?"

He'd been waiting for her. That pleased her, though she didn't know why it should.

"Gorgeous."

He stepped back to allow plenty of room for her to pass through and looked down at her armload of books. "Can I carry those for you?"

"No, thanks. I'm used to lugging them around."

Her eyes adjusted from the brightness outside to the inside lighting as she surveyed the reception area—textured off-white wallpaper, lush cream-colored carpet, leather sofa and chairs, nautical pictures matted and framed in driftwood, the dark green of tropical plants splashed at strategic points. The decor projected a prestigious image, she mused, and yet there was also what a native-born Texan would call a down-home flavor.

"Pleasant business quarters," she commented. "Did Leslie Faye help decorate?"

"As a matter of fact, she did." He gestured toward the woman seated at the desk. "Alana Benton, Carmela Delgado."

His secretary's warm smile was the finishing touch the office needed. Alana shifted her books to her left arm and extended her hand. "Nice to meet you. I must have spoken to you earlier on the phone."

Carmela nodded. "My pleasure. Can I get you a cup of coffee or tea?"

"No, but thanks for offering."

"Would you hold my calls until after lunch?" Sylas asked Carmela. "Miss Benton and I will be in consultation." He gestured for Alana to precede him down the short hallway. "First door on the right. Gregory's office is on the left. The bathroom is the door at the end of the hallway."

She glanced to the left as she passed Gregory's office.

"He's at the courthouse this morning," Sylas said, reaching in front of her to open his office door. "He won't be joining us today."

"At breakfast, Leslie Faye mentioned that Gregory was taking her into Houston for lunch." She had also commented on his taking her to more places since their divorce than while they were married. "She was looking forward to it."

Inside Kincaid's office, Alana took the chair Sylas motioned toward while he circled behind his desk. She glanced at the small sofa and chair in the corner of his office and wondered if he'd purposely put the desk between them as a signal that she was in his domain and he was the boss.

When she returned her attention to him, he'd leaned back in his chair and was looking at her thoughtfully. She also noticed that the missing books were now neatly stacked at one corner of his desk.

Sylas watched Alana while she familiarized herself with his office. It wasn't as prosperous looking as the reception area or as showy as Gregory's office. He knew that. But he considered the furnishings and atmosphere conducive to getting the job done. He saw her nod, as though she had made her own conclusions.

"I see you absconded with the books you suggested I read," she said lightly, a bit discomfited by his steady gray eyes. She had the feeling he was trying to get inside her head to see what made her tick. "Shall we trade reading material?"

He picked up the top book on the stack; his finger worried across the block-lettered title. "You said you haven't worked on a case of this nature. Correct?"

"Correct."

She broke eye contact by placing her purse next to her chair on the floor. She wondered how he'd react if she said, I don't need to read the books. I've experienced it. Undoubtedly his jaw would drop to his chest and he'd be appropriately sympathetic. Until I left, she added. Then he'd start wondering what kind of woman I am. Am I the type of woman who enticed and teased a man, then cried rape when things went too far?

She straightened until her spine was rigid against the back of the chair. She wouldn't give him cause to wonder about her; she wouldn't tell him anything. He had read the books. Let him do the talking.

Sylas opened the cover and flipped through the pages. "Last night Leslie Faye mentioned that you'd thought at first she'd been grabbed and forced into an alley. That's pretty much what I assumed until I found out the circumstances." He skimmed the page, looking at the notations he'd made in the margin. "Did you know that one in four women on college campuses are victims of rape or attempted rape?"

Alana swallowed. She could feel her heartbeat accelerate. Her fingers clutched the wooden arms of the chair.

He doesn't know, she silently droned. No one knows!

"According to the statistics in this book, eighty-four percent of the women knew their attacker and fifty-seven percent of the rapes happened on dates. What amazes me is that most of these women didn't report the incident to the police. Some of them didn't even consider it rape."

While he read, Alana concentrated on getting control of herself. Finger by finger she released her grip. Her palms felt cold and clammy. She resisted the impulse to wipe them on her skirt. Instead, she propped her elbows on the end of the arms of the chair and lightly placed both hands on her kneecap. All the while, she practiced what the woman at the airport had told her to do by steadily inhaling and exhaling.

Sylas glanced across the desk to see if these statistics surprised Alana as much as they'd amazed him.

"Leslie Faye had dated Ed Morgan," she said. Her voice sounded tight, strained, to her own ears, but Sylas appeared not to notice.

He nodded, then leaned back as he pulled a legal pad from the center drawer. "These were college students who were surveyed, but it scares the hell out of me to think they might be voicing their parents' attitudes—the people who could be on Leslie Faye's jury."

"We'll conduct our own survey." Alana avoided looking at Kincaid. The room seemed to have warmed ten degrees. "Different locales often produce different results."

"Listen to this," Sylas said, skimming down through a list of notes he'd gathered from newspaper and magazine articles. "A woman who gets raped probably deserves it, especially if she's been drinking." He shook his head. "Women who don't fight back haven't been raped. If she isn't a virgin then she isn't a victim." His forefinger tapped the next sentence he'd written. "Here's a doozer. If a woman lets a man buy her dinner or pay for drinks and movie tickets, then she owes him sex."

Alana's throat worked to keep the bile from rising farther. Was that what people said? Poor Leslie Faye. At least Alana had been able to keep her shame a secret.

"Uh, do you think it would be possible for me to get a drink of water, or maybe a Coke?"

"Sure." He stabbed the button on the intercom and made the request to Carmela. Observing how pale Alana had become, he said, "It's the humidity that gets you. I swear, there are days when I can't decide whether I'm perspiring or the water in the air is condensing on my skin."

She appreciated his mild attempt at humor to relieve her discomfort. She forced the corners of her mouth to lift a fraction of an inch. The last sentence he'd read off his legal pad had sent her stomach into a spin. Had Tom thought a hamburger and fries constituted payment for sexual favors? If what had happened hadn't been such a personal tragedy, the idea of exchanging fast food for sex would have been almost laughable.

Laughable? She wanted to cry.

"You could give your body a chance to adjust," Sylas suggested, "by reading these books while you laze around the beach."

"No, I'm only thirsty." As long as there was someone with her, she had to maintain control over her emotions. "Go on with your notes. What else do people believe?"

Sylas considered arguing with her. At first he'd thought her uneasiness was caused by discussing this topic with someone she'd just met, but some of the court cases she'd worked on previously ranged from brutal murders to child abuse. Comparatively speaking, his notes were tame stuff.

"Okay. Once a man is aroused he can't help forcing sex on a woman."

"Is that true?"

"I don't subscribe to the uncontrollable-urge theory." He strummed his fingers impatiently on his desk, wondering what was keeping Carmela. Alana wasn't the only one who needed a drink of water.

"Then a man can stop at any point?"

"He can't stop if he's recently had a lobotomy and his brain isn't functioning properly," Sylas answered dryly. He shifted position. "I think sex for both men and women is mental as well as physical." He tapped his temple with one finger. "What's going on up here is what make sex great, don't you agree?"

Alana inwardly cringed, but outwardly, she nodded in agreement. "Yeah. Sure. I just didn't know if men felt the same way women did."

"I can't back up that statement with statistics. That was personal opinion."

"Do you think women provoke rape by how they dress or things they say?"

"Leslie Faye isn't the type to wear tight sweaters or to make vulgar suggestions to a man."

"Are you dodging the question, counselor?"

"No. I was relating the question to the case."

Carmela knocked softly, then entered the office. Sylas rose and took the tray of soft drinks and ice bucket from her. "Thanks."

"What about hip-hugging blue jeans? Miniskirts? String bikinis?" Alana asked.

He filled a glass with ice, twisted the cap off a Coke and poured the liquid down the side. "A man notices them, but unless he's been living in a cave without a television, radio or newspaper, he should realize women follow fashion trends."

Alana took the drink as she mulled over his answer in her mind. Back in college her casual wardrobe had consisted of jeans, sweatshirts and boots. She bit her lip to stop herself from blurting Tom's graphic description of her clothing.

Kincaid had researched the subject, she reminded herself. He'd said the type of clothing a woman wore did not incite a man's lust beyond the point of no return.

Then maybe, she silently speculated, just maybe what happened wasn't my fault?

But she couldn't accept that possibility. To start with, she'd used poor judgment. She'd been irresponsible and naive. Stupid, she silently condemned. She should have fought off the attack, screamed for help, escaped. She'd done none of the three.

The blame rested squarely on her shoulders.

A dull throb that had begun at the base of her neck had traveled to the crown of her head. Unless she took some aspirin immediately, she knew tension and stress would cause a cluster headache within hours.

"Alana?"

Reflexively, her head snapped upward. A shard of pain hit her between the eyes, but she saw Sylas holding out a glass to her. "Oh, yes. Thanks."

She put the glass to her lips and gulped the fizzy liquid. While the beverage burned its way across her tongue and down her throat, she reached for her purse.

Sylas watched her remove two tablets from her purse. Parallel lines of stress were etched between her eyebrows. He glanced at the digital clock on his desk. Almost noon. "Headache?"

"Mmm." Alana placed the tablets on her tongue, drank a sip, then tilted her head back.

"Did you eat breakfast?"

She shook her head and swallowed. "Coffee."

"Aspirin on an empty stomach? You don't have much regard for your stomach lining, do you?" he muttered, circling his desk. "C'mon, let's go feed that headache."

"We've barely started. Lunch can wait."

"You aren't one of those Type A people who run themselves ragged working and don't eat properly, are you?"

"No." Her hand covered her mouth to conceal the white lie. Sylas stood entirely too close to her chair, hovering over her. "I eat when I'm hungry."

"Well, it's nearly noon and I'm hungry." He started to put his hand on the back of her chair, but the way she shifted to one side away from him halted his movement. He straightened his shoulders and stepped backward, not offering her his hand. At some point very soon, he silently promised himself, he was going to tell her that rejecting his deeply ingrained courtesies was extremely offensive to him. For now, he said, "I'm going out for lunch. If you want to stay here and pop pills to get rid of your headache, you go right ahead."

Alana lithely rose from the chair, gathering her purse in her arm. There was a time to fight and a time to give in gracefully.

"Where?"

"The Hotel Galvez has a good luncheon buffet."

"It's been restored?"

Sylas grinned, relaxing the muscle along his jaw. He moved toward the door. "Yeah, it has. I keep forgetting you haven't been around for a while. I think you'll like it."

Ten minutes later, they strolled through the hotel lobby. Alana had the distinct feeling they'd stepped back to the turn of the century. Everything, from the carpeting to the chandeliers overhead, had been meticulously rejuvenated. She glanced down at her dress, thinking that a long gown with a bustle and a matching ruffled parasol were all she needed to complete the picture.

Sylas touched her elbow to guide her toward the dining area.

Automatically Alana drew her arm closer to her waist.

"Stop it," Sylas murmured. He softened his command with a winsome smile.

"Stop what?"

"Shrinking away from me when I casually touch you." Again, he tried to soften what he'd said, this time with a joke. "My parents spent years training me in the fine art of gentlemanly social graces. You wouldn't want me to disappoint them, would you?"

"I promise not to mention it," Alana replied, suddenly uncertain whether her defensive mechanisms weren't part of the emotional scar tissue around her heart. To veer away from the subject, she asked, "Do they live in Galveston?"

"No, ma'am," he drawled, "they're ranchers in west Texas."

"Good afternoon, folks. Welcome to the Galvez," the maître d' said in greeting. "Two?"

Sylas nodded. "The buffet."

Following the host, Alana felt her mouth water as they passed by a long table filled with seafood delicacies, a standing rib roast and side dishes of vegetables. An ice carving of a swan graced the end of the table.

"Would you care for a drink?" Sylas inquired after they'd been seated.

"Iced tea." Remembering that Southern restaurants often sweetened this beverage before serving it, she added, "Without sugar. Double lemon on the side, please."

"Very well," said the maître d'.

"I'll have mine sweetened, no lemon."

"You're welcome to go to the buffet when you're ready. Jack will be your waiter should you need anything else."

"I'm ready when you are," Sylas said to Alana, thinking the sooner she had something in her stomach the sooner she'd feel better.

"Fine." Aware that he would pull her chair back for her, Alana tried not to flinch when she felt his hands within inches of her shoulders. "Thank you."

"Thank *you*," he teased.

When they returned to the table, Sylas dropped his napkin on his lap, waiting, while Alana unfolded and spread her napkin over her lap, for her to pick up her fork. Silently he compared his heaping plate to hers, which held small samplings of several dishes that looked as though they'd been measured to be identical amounts. He also noted her food was arranged neatly around her plate, like the numbers on a clock, which he presumed was to keep one flavor from blending with another.

Neat and tidy, Sylas mused silently, like her clothing, her hair and probably her mind. Compartmentalized. Regimented. Nothing touching, nothing blending. His lips quirked in amusement as he mentally wagered that she'd wield her fork clockwise around the plate.

"Care to let me in on the joke?" Alana asked, her fork poised above the creamy carrot and raisin salad.

"I just made a private bet."

"On what?"

"The order you'd eat your food."

She glanced downward.

"I'd also bet that when you go to the grocery store, your list matches the aisles." He openly grinned. "When you get to the checkout, the canned goods and bottles are in rows on the bottom of the cart and the fresh fruit and veggies are on top."

She thought about it and grinned. "You're right. But wouldn't it be imprudent to handpick a tomato and then squash it under a gallon of milk?"

"Yeah. Messy, too."

He cut a small piece of meat, forked it into his mouth and savored the taste before chewing it.

Alana's eyes bounced from the delighted expression on his face to his plate. Meat and potatoes, with three scoops of unidentifiable dishes that she'd avoided.

"What is that concoction on the far side of your plate?"

"This?" He pointed with his fork. "It's Passion Fruit Delight. Want to try it?"

"What's in it?"

"Papaya, mango, pineapple and kiwifruit, mixed with whipped cream. Some kind of juice makes the whipped cream pink. It tastes great." Without thinking, he offered her some on his fork. "Try it."

"Maybe later."

Not offended, Sylas ate the bite, shifting it to one side of his mouth as he said, "After ten o'clock, huh?"

Alana grinned. "I've heard of two-hour lunches, but I don't plan on being here that long."

Chuckling, Sylas directed her gaze to her plate by nodding his head. "Your food is arranged like a clock.

After ten is between the slices of fresh fruit, the sweet flavors, you plan on ending your meal with.''

Sylas paused, waiting to see if Alana was too uptight to laugh at her little idiosyncrasy. Mentally, he scored a point in her favor as he listened to her laughter.

Dare he push her an inch further?

Impulsively, deciding he should, he excused himself, returning to the buffet table to get Alana a small dish of Passion Fruit Delight.

''Be adventuresome,'' he said, placing the dish to the right of her plate. ''Try something you've never eaten before, and eat it at three o'clock, for a change.''

Alana heard the teasing challenge in his voice. Sylas Kincaid was definitely a scoundrel—a nice sort of scoundrel. No wonder Leslie Faye liked him. They were two of a kind.

She tasted the unfamiliar food. The combination of sweetness and tartness was pleasing to her palate. ''It is good.''

Her concessions pleased Sylas. He considered insisting that she taste the other two foods on his plate that she'd avoided but when he noticed that she'd returned to eating in her usual order, he decided to wait until another day. He guessed she was a woman willing to try new things, but only on a limited basis.

Sylas figured his patience could outlast her cautiousness.

''I think I'm going to run into one major problem in Leslie Faye's defense when I introduce the date rape issue,'' Sylas said later the same afternoon, after Alana had read through pages of his notes while he read the material she'd given him. ''Lack of evidence. Ed Morgan has a scar on his face. A juror will be able to see it plainly. It proves he was assaulted. He'll testify that she exploded when he told her he wouldn't be asking her out again, and hit him. I don't have any tangible proof Leslie Faye was defending herself."

Alana tapped her pencil on the papers she'd been reading. Although she shuddered at the idea, she had to admit that photographs or hospital documentation of physical violence would have strengthened her friend's case.

"What we'll have to do is prove Leslie Faye isn't prone to physical violence," she said. "During jury selection, we'll have her direct an open-ended question to one of the prospective jurors regarding psychological versus physical abuse."

"I know it's customary in the cases you handle for the defendant to direct questions, but in this case..."

She tossed her pencil on the papers. "Yes?"

"I don't think she's up to it."

"It's important for her to make verbal contact with the jurors. When they answer her direct questions, she's no longer just a warm body occupying the courtroom. She's a living, breathing person. Someone they can relate to."

"Will they relate to someone who falls apart in the middle of a question?"

"Leslie Faye won't fall apart. Believe me, the lady has plenty of fortitude."

He looked at her briefly, then looked away toward a magazine on his desk top, as he folded his arms across his chest.

He's made up his mind, Alana quickly interpreted. To continue trying to convince him would be futile. She'd have to coach Leslie Faye, then show Sylas the results before he would allow his client to take an active part in the jury selection process.

She reached for the magazine, instantly recognizing the cover. From his frown, she deduced there was something in the article about her that worried him. His look didn't tell her the entire story of what was going on in his mind.

"Tell me what you're thinking," she coaxed.

"You don't want to know what I'm thinking."

"Let me decide that. It's apparent you don't like this magazine for some reason. What is it?"

Sylas hesitated. He preferred not answering her question directly. "I don't dislike the magazine. I don't often read it. Somebody gave that copy to me."

"Oh? Who?"

"Gregory."

"Was there something in particular he wanted you to read?"

She wasn't going to drop the subject. He knew it. She knew it.

"Yes."

"The article about me?" she guessed.

"As a matter of fact, yes." Sylas felt like a thief caught with his hand in a cash register who was trying to make explanations to the store owner. "Leslie Faye gave him a stack of magazines to read about you."

Now she was getting somewhere. There was only one reason she could think of for Leslie Faye to have done that—she'd been attempting to convince Gregory that Alana could help her case.

Alana felt fairly certain, from Kincaid's reluctance to discuss the article, that Gregory's reason for showing it to Kincaid wasn't to extol her virtues in the courtroom.

"I'm not going to quote Gregory again and have you say, 'Bully for you.'" He refused to meet her eyes.

"Fine. Don't quote Gregory. Tell me what worries you."

"The same thing that worries me whenever I take a new case. Am I representing someone guilty or someone innocent? I don't think you care if John Doe committed a felony."

His admitting they had a common problem made her reply less difficult to express. "I do care, but I also care about John Doe getting a fair trial. Our judicial system is nothing but a cruel joke if the defendant isn't promised fairness. I don't want twelve people to render a decision based on gender or race or creed."

She ruffled the corners of his legal pad. "Or to make their decision based on misbegotten, Victorian attitudes. In Leslie Faye's particular case, for instance, the majority of her peers won't believe her. It's my job to sift through the juror information sheets they fill out, to watch them, to listen to their answers and to eliminate the chance of a biased person being in the position to cast a ballet against someone who is innocent."

A curt voice cut in from the hallway. "And while you're saving the innocent, you don't mind making one hell of a name for yourself as a side benefit, do you?" Gregory strode into the office as though he belonged there.

Alana twisted in her chair. Behind her, she heard the front legs of Kincaid's chair sink into the carpet.

"You don't see Paid Advertisement printed in small letters at the bottom of the article, do you?"

"No, but you wouldn't mind seeing your face plastered on the cover of the *Texas Monthly*. Leslie Faye's trial is a matter of open record, but I prefer not to have her exploited for your personal benefit. This case means nothing more to you than a high-stake five card stud game, with you watching everybody's expression and guessing what they have in their hands. Instead of playing your cards close to your chest, why don't you spread your cards on the table?''

Sylas rose to his feet. He planted his fists on his desk, leaned forward and said harshly, ''That's enough, Gregory.''

''No, Sylas. I appreciate your jumping to my defense, but I'm capable of handling this myself,'' Alana said, turning from Kincaid to Gregory.

Using his analogy, she knew Gregory thought he held a pat hand. But she also knew two-thirds of his bravado was nothing but bluff. Figuratively, she had two aces showing—Leslie Faye and Kincaid wanted her on the case. What Gregory didn't know was that she had an ace in the hole. She removed a folded document from her attaché case, stood up and slowly walked toward him. She spread the page as though she were spreading her cards on a table.

''Read this and weep, Gregory.'' She turned her back on him, gathered her belongings along with several of Kincaid's books and strode toward the door, head held high. ''If you'll excuse me, it's been a long day. I'll finish reading this material tonight.''

Before she closed the door behind her, she said, ''And by the way, gentlemen. I noticed yesterday that neither of you can say 'rape' in Leslie Faye's presence. Since she will be in the courtroom, I suggest you practice saying it.''

Chapter Five

I'll tell you what, Sylas. Alana Benton has more nerve than Washington, D.C., has politicians." Gregory tossed the sheet of paper Alana had given him on the desk. "I ask her if she plans on exploiting this case and what does she hand me? A document that *I'm* supposed to sign stating that *Hale and Kincaid* won't contact the media!"

Without a moment's hesitation, Sylas picked up a pen and signed the document. "You noticed that she signed a similar agreement in the bottom paragraph, didn't you?"

Gregory had moved to the window overlooking the Gulf and had begun muttering to himself. "I never liked her. She was always telling Leslie Faye when to jump and how high. I swear, I think the woman must be some sort of a voodoo curse someone put on me!"

"What are you grumbling about? Alana agreed to what you wanted and you're still griping." He crossed to stand beside Gregory. "Speaking of agreements, when you and I went into partnership, we agreed to have complete autonomy on our individual cases. You assigned Leslie Faye's case to me."

"So?"

"I won't have you antagonizing Alana Benton while we're working on the case."

Gregory raised one hand to stop Sylas from going any further. "This is different. Leslie Faye is my wife."

"Ex-wife."

"Okay. Ex-wife, but I still have a vested interest in the case."

"You have choices. Butt out or contact another attorney or take the case to trial yourself."

"I can't represent her in court." His hand dropped impotently to his side. "You know I can't. Dammit, man, I only want what's best for Leslie Faye!"

"That leaves two choices remaining. Which is it?"

"You." He ruffled his fingers through his short blond hair. "I'll butt out."

"And?"

"Okay. I'll keep quiet around Alana. She's all yours." Gregory turned toward the desk, removing his gold pen from his breast pocket. "I still say she has a lot of nerve asking us to sign this."

"I'm certain she has her reasons." Sylas hadn't the vaguest notion what those reasons were, but then, he wasn't as meticulous as Alana. She'd proved that point at lunch.

"I hate to admit this, but I took one of her suggestions. I hired a private detective to investigate Ed Morgan." Gregory signed the document, and put the cap back on his pen. "I think it's pointless. If he's been involved in this sort of thing before, the police would know about it."

"Not necessarily," Sylas commented, thinking of the women who were too ashamed to file charges. "Not necessarily."

Alana was sitting cross-legged in the center of her bed, with papers and books in a semicircle around her, when Leslie Faye knocked on her bedroom door. She'd changed from her dress into a loose-fitting jogging shirt, azure blue, with a fluffy lining that felt good against her bare skin.

"Come in," she called, adding a notation in the margin of a text on the aftereffects of date rape. She looked up as her friend entered.

"Gregory invited me over to his house for dinner. There's a salad in the refrigerator and spaghetti on the stove. Do you mind if I go?" Leslie Faye asked.

"Uh-uh." Alana chewed on the eraser of her pencil, trying to put Leslie Faye in one of the classifications she'd read. She simply didn't fit! "Do you mind my asking a couple of personal questions?"

Leslie Faye chuckled. "Since when would my minding stop you. Fire away!"

"How did Gregory react to all of this?"

"He wanted to meet Ed at dawn under an oak tree with dueling pistols."

"Be serious," Alana chided.

"He wanted to go over to his house and knock his block off, but I stopped him."

Alana could believe Gregory would react explosively. What she truly wanted to know was how he'd reacted toward Leslie Faye. "Did he blame you for what happened?"

"I think mostly he blames himself. He knows I dated a lot after the divorce, but he also knows I didn't sleep around." Leslie Faye nervously adjusted the silk scarf she wore at the neckline of her paisley print jumpsuit. "He says this never would have happened if he'd stopped me from filing for divorce."

"Could he have stopped you?"

"Yeah. A little attention would have gone a long way toward filling the gap between us."

Alana nodded. "He's filling that gap now, isn't he? Does that mean the two of you might get back together?"

"I can't see him married to a convict."

Leslie Faye's sad smile touched Alana's heart. Her friend's hopes were pinned to the outcome of this trial. Alana watched her chin wobble. She opened her arms. Oblivious to the books and papers on the bed, Leslie Faye hurled herself into Alana's embrace.

"It's going to be okay," Alana reassured her, hugging her tightly. "We're doing our best to prevent that from happening."

Leslie Faye sniffed and tried to smile. She brushed her curly hair from her face, then touched Alana's sleek hair. "You can wear a pin-striped suit and look great. I'd look lousy in wide black-and-white stripes."

To humor her friend, Alana said, "I'd look like a bean pole wrapped in tissue paper."

"A feminine bean pole with bumps in all the right places. I used to curse myself for choosing the best-looking girl in high school to be my best friend. The guys always asked you out before they noticed me."

"That's not true," Alana protested, both surprised and flattered. She hugged her a second time. "But thanks for feeding my ego."

"It is true. It's those big brown eyes of yours. And your hair. Good looks and brains." Leslie Faye groaned. "I didn't stand a chance with a guy if he met you first. That's why you didn't meet Gregory until after I had his fraternity pin."

"You didn't have anything to worry about with him," Alana said, softly chuckling. "He took one look at me and instantly disliked me."

"I hate to admit it, but that was one of the things going in his favor." She lowered her face, then peeked at Alana through a thick fringe of eyelashes. "I love him, Alana. Then and now. I do kind of wish you'd get along better with him. He really has been good to me since the Morgan thing."

Alana loved her friend and would have done anything for her, but she couldn't make rash promises about Gregory. As far back as she could remember, she had found Gregory abrasive.

"I said I'm willing to call a truce . . . if he is." That was the best Alana could offer. "I won't let him take swipes at me professionally without giving as good as I get."

"Can I tell him that?" Leslie Faye bounced off the bed.

"For all the good it will do you," Alana muttered. Gregory Hale would rather eat Texas-size rattle-snakes than act friendly toward her.

Leslie Faye was halfway out the door when she spun around. "And Alana . . . thanks for the hugs. I needed them."

"Me, too," she answered, but Leslie Faye was gone before she'd spoken.

One of the case histories she'd read earlier in the evening dealt with the reactions of family and friends to one particular date rape victim. On a couple of occasions the woman, whom the author had called Susan, had confided in her friends. After that, not one of those friends wanted to be around her, because knowing it could happen to Susan meant it might happen to them, too. The thought of a "nice, respectable man," someone they knew, being sexually violent came too close. It could happen to them, and they didn't want to face that possibility. In addition, Susan's own mother had felt as though her "little girl" had been ruined.

What happened to Susan was exactly what Alana had feared would happen to her. Ashamed of herself for using such poor judgment, she couldn't have tolerated her friends being standoffish. Nor had she wanted to be on the receiving end of pitying glances.

If Leslie Faye had known her best friend was a victim, and if she'd responded in typical fashion, their friendship would have died, then and there. Leslie Faye wouldn't have been able to ask for Alana's help.

"You made the right decision," she murmured aloud. She wrapped her arms around herself. What was that old saying about hindsight having twenty-twenty vision? Now that her trauma was over, it was easy to say she'd done the right thing. What other choices had there been?

She reclined against the headboard, wondering what her life would have been like if she hadn't been attacked. Would she have married? Probably. She might have had two or three children.

She wouldn't be a jury consultant. Too much travel for a wife and mother. Too much pressure.

No, she'd probably have chosen a different area of law.

Her mind circled back to her first question. Whom would she have married? There hadn't been anyone special even before the incident with Tom. But she knew what she'd wanted in a man. Looks didn't mean much. Since she was above average height for a woman, she'd liked her dates to be more than six feet tall. She'd wanted someone with common interests, someone she could talk to, someone she could rely on.

Had she met anyone who fit those criteria that she'd passed by because . . . ?

Alana closed her eyes and pressed her lips tightly together. She wasn't willing to admit she'd evaded having a personal relationship with a man because . . .

A shiver ran up her back and across her shoulders.

Was she afraid it would happen again?

Alana rocked her head from side to side against the headboard. She wasn't afraid, not after all these years.

Even without the information she'd crammed into her head during the past twelve hours, she knew she wouldn't be a victim of poor judgment again. She was careful. She listened to the little voice inside of her that said, "Watch out. Be cautious."

Was there such a thing as being too careful?

She was still pondering the possibility drowsily when the doorbell rang. Her eyes snapped open. She unfolded her legs, swung them over the side of the bed and crossed to the door.

She checked to make certain Leslie Faye had locked the door, then called, "Who is it?"

"Pizza delivery."

"I didn't order a pizza."

"Would you be interested in a free pizza? Large. Piping hot."

Alana recognized the teasing quality perpetually in Sylas Kincaid's voice. She glanced at the mirrored tiles on the foyer wall. Although she appeared fully clothed, Alana knew she lacked proper underclothing.

"Kincaid?" she asked, stalling, "Is that you?"

"Yes. Open the door. This pizza box is hot!"

Alana bit her lips. She raised her hand to unlock the door, then dropped it back to her side. Twice.

"Should I slide the hot, steaming pizza with everything on it except anchovies, under the door? Or are you going to open it?"

The tiny voice in the back of her head must have been under a gag order. It was strangely silent.

"Just a minute."

Hot pizza or cold dog chow, tiny voice or no tiny voice, she knew better than to invite a man into her lodgings, especially when she wasn't decently clothed.

She fumbled with the dead-bolt lock as though trying to unlock it.

"Is the lock stuck?"

"Uh..." Her innate truthfulness wouldn't let a bold-faced lie slip through her lips.

Sylas shifted the pizza box from one hand to the other. Damn! His fingers would be cremated by the time she unlocked the door!

Suddenly, it crossed his mind that Alana might not open the door. A woman who arranged her food on her plate and wouldn't let a man within a foot of her was not the sort of woman who enjoyed unexpected company.

"Alana?"

"Yeah?"

"I called over to Gregory's house and Leslie Faye said she felt guilty about leaving you alone at dinner-time. She said you were busy reading through a stack of books. I hate eating alone, so I thought it would be a friendly gesture to drop by with a pizza. I just realized you're probably feeling uneasy about letting in someone you scarcely know when you're alone."

When he voiced her inner fears, Alana thought they sounded damned silly. She'd been with him in his office most of the day. Granted, the door had been ajar and Carmela had been within shouting distance, but nevertheless he hadn't made a pass at her.

If she sent him away, he'd think she didn't trust him. Leslie Faye trusted him to win her freedom. Gregory trusted him as a business partner. Of course, she didn't put much faith in Gregory's opinion. She'd have felt better if Gregory detested him.

One for, one against, she deliberated. She had to cast the swing vote.

She could trust Kincaid, couldn't she?

Alana had less faith in her own judgment than she had in Gregory's. But she did have faith in the warning voice inside her head that alerted her to danger. She'd heard it and ignored it when she was going up to Tom's room. She wasn't hearing a peep from it now.

Sylas stooped and placed the pizza box on the plank floor. He'd looked forward to sharing it, but what the hell, he'd be nervous, too, under similar circumstances. Next time he'd call first.

"Enjoy the pizza. Don't work too hard. I'll see you tomorrow morning."

"Wait!" Impulsively, Alana turned the latch. "Count to twenty, slowly, then come inside."

Alana sped through the living room into the bedroom, slamming the door and twisting the lock. Her heart pounded as though it had been replaced by an angry judge's gavel. She put her hands over it to muffle the accelerated beating.

After counting to fifty, Sylas opened the door and crossed to the kitchen table. He assumed Alana had gone into her room to do whatever it was that women did to prepare for a male guest.

"Is it okay if I get some Cokes out of the refrigerator?"

"Help yourself." Her voice sounded high-pitched, louder than it should have been. "I'll be out in a minute."

An hour, she silently corrected. Maybe tomorrow morning? By then he would have disappeared.

Or be knocking on the bedroom door.

That thought gave her impetus. She raced to the dresser, yanked open the top drawer and dug through her lingerie until she found a bra. She unzipped the front placket of her jogging suit and swore it sounded as though she'd ripped through a piece of cloth. She shrugged out of it, then into her bra.

"Don't panic!" she coached in a whisper. Her fingers shook; she couldn't get the hooks into the eyes. She slouched her shoulders until the shoulder straps were off. Turning her bra until the hooks and eyes were in front, she fastened them, then tugged at the elastic until it was in its proper place.

The small accomplishment gave her the same feeling she had when a client was acquitted.

"If he tries anything, this time you'll scream the whole damn building down around his ears."

She glanced at the zippered top she'd tossed on the floor and shook her head. Too easy. She opened the bottom drawer and found a fleece sweatshirt ... with a tight neck.

He'll never get this off, she assured herself.

He won't try.

Alana cocked her head to one side. Unable to accept what she'd heard from her small inner voice, she retorted silently, He's a man, isn't he?

She waited, listening for a reply, listening for advice. She heard only the sound of Sylas opening the Coke bottles.

Dead certain that at least fifteen or twenty minutes had passed, she glanced at her watch as she picked up a brush to tidy her hair. She brushed it back from her face, clasping it at her nape with one hand as she reached into the top drawer to get a hair clasp.

Alana silently groaned. In her scramble to find her bra, she'd left the drawer in complete disarray. She pushed her clothes from one side to the other, but the hair clasp was nowhere to be found.

What a woman wears or what she looks like doesn't matter, she thought, remembering what Kincaid had said along with what she'd read. A man doesn't have a lust button that gets pushed by the sight of a short skirt or long hair.

She dropped the brush on the dresser in defeat.

"Okay. We'll test their theory. He touches my hair—I start screaming."

She knew she was being irrational, but since her warning signals were malfunctioning, she couldn't expect to be rational. She swiped her palms down the side of her pants, took a long deep breath to sustain her for the next hour or so and walked toward the door—slowly, as though an executioner awaited her on the other side.

Chapter Six

I hope you like your pizza with everything," Sylas said, rising as she entered the dinette area. "I tried to get them to fix each slice with a different topping—so they weren't mixed together—but the manager said no." Her mouth barely lifted at the corners, but he wasn't dissuaded. "He did offer to fix sixteen small pizzas at a reduced price, though."

"It smells good." She took the chair Sylas held for her. The blended aroma of pepperoni, onions, green peppers and pizza-manager-only-knew-what-else smelled heavenly. "I have a weakness for Italian food. In St. Louis I go to the Italian section called the Hill at least once a week. One restaurant fixes homemade ravioli, served with melted butter on the side. It's absolutely fantastic."

She knew she was chattering about nothing; she couldn't stop. Over a thick crust piled high with toppings, she ventured a fleeting glance at Sylas. He'd changed clothes. Gone were the expensive gray suit, white shirt and silk tie. Tonight his clothes were as casual as his dropping by with a pizza. His gray pullover shirt exactly matched his gray eyes. His slacks looked worn, comfortable.

She had to admit silently that she liked a man who wore his clothes with ease.

Her eyes met his.

He smiled.

Her cheeks turned a rosy pink. Knowing she'd been caught eyeing him, she covered up being flustered by raising her verbal barrier again.

"St. Louis is known for its ethnic celebrations... Hill Day, the Badenfest, the Greek Festival..." She pulled a slice of pizza from the box. Strings of cheese stuck to the cardboard. With one finger she wound the strings until they broke. "But my favorite place for pizza is in Charleston, South Carolina. Down at the Market Place. This sounds awful, but they make the best shrimp, ham and pineapple pizza in the world."

Her nonstop monologue reminded Sylas of a toy soldier he'd had as a kid. Wound up tightly, the tiny replica of a general would march, swing its arms and salute at the same pace as Alana's mouth.

"Alana, eat, before it freezes in your hand. Pizza Popsicles are terrible."

"I am eating. What about you?" She thought she might have accidentally found a means to end her one-woman show. Given the opportunity, men loved to talk about themselves. "Why aren't you over at your girlfriend's house eating pizza with her?"

"Because I'm presently unattached. Is there someone special in your life?"

Alana shook her head and continued chewing. While he patiently waited for her to elucidate, she swallowed. "Travel and a social life don't mix. Were you ever...attached?"

The slightest hint of a twinkle he saw in her eyes was enough to make Sylas chuckle. "You twisted my word, didn't you?"

She grinned.

"I was attached. Once. Kate O'Donnell. Our parents owned adjoining land."

"Very convenient."

"I'll admit to my father having a hopeful gleam in his eye, but I knew I didn't want to be a rancher. My younger brother, John, has an affinity for the land." Sylas watched Alana devour the crust of her first piece of pizza and reach for another. "Kate and I had been friends so long we thought we were in love. We discussed everything from who'd be invited to our wedding to what color hair our firstborn would have. But we came to find out we were in love with love, not each other."

"Oh?"

"Umm. The relationship did lead to marriage, though—hers to another man. I guess both of us knew all along that we'd be better friends than marriage partners, otherwise I don't think she'd have fallen head over heels in love with the first stranger who moved to town—a law school buddy of mine." With the dramatic flair of a trial lawyer, he thumped his chest. "But deep in here, I knew I was the best man...the groom's best man at Kate's wedding."

Mouth full, Alana made a comical face at his twisting the meaning of another word.

"And I'm the father of her first child. The godfather."

Alana felt her heart go out to Sylas. He could joke about the woman he'd cared for marrying another man, but she felt certain he wasn't as casual about it as he was trying to lead her to believe.

She ventured, "You must still be in love with her if you aren't dating anyone."

"I'm not that unattached. I didn't say I wasn't dating." With a devilish wink, he chuckled as he asked, "Care to give a shot at mending my broken heart?"

She laughed with him. "Bigamy isn't my style."

"I thought Leslie Faye said you weren't married." His eyes dropped to her bare ring finger.

"Not in her sense of the word. To me, marriage means total commitment. I am committed."

"To your job?"

She nodded, pleased with his keen perception. She polished off the second slice and took a long drink of Coke. "Happily married. I don't need a man mucking around in my life."

With equal candor, Sylas said, " I get lonely. Don't you?"

"No." Alana covered her mouth with her napkin, wiping her lips. "Never."

Sylas, having read the book about body language she'd lent him, recognized the traitorous gesture. She's fibbing, he mused, wondering if she'd convinced herself she was never lonely or if she was trying to convince him of that fact. "Never?"

"Rarely," she finally admitted. "I keep busy."

"Drawing up no-publicity documents for attorneys to sign?" Sylas teased. "You certainly spiked Gregory's cannon."

Alana wadded the napkin in her lap. She had private reasons for not wanting her whereabouts known. A cold chill ran up her spine as she remembered Tom repeatedly calling her before she'd left for Missouri, asking her to go out with him! No, she hadn't been thinking of Gregory when she wrote the agreement. She simply wasn't taking any chances on Tom discovering she'd returned to Galveston.

As he'd spoken, Sylas had witnessed her looking away to the corner of the room. Was she signaling that she didn't want him to know what she felt? That she felt cornered? She crossed her legs at the knees. Another clue that she'd shut him out. New to the body language theories, he wondered if he was interpreting her actions correctly.

During their short acquaintanceship, she'd always appeared confident and self-assured, and yet here, now, there was something about her that made her seem vulnerable. Appealing. Some intangible force made him want to reach out and touch her.

Alana reached for another slice of pizza. Her wrist grazed against the back of his hand. Before she separated the slices, his thumb and forefinger circled her wrist.

"I'm sorry I brought up Gregory's name." He flicked her a brief smile when she looked up at him. "I want you to know he won't come barging into my private office again. When it comes to him and Leslie Faye's case, it's strictly hands-off from now on. Okay?"

Her eyes dropped to where he touched her. Except for the light hold he had on her his other fingers were relaxed and open. Instinctively she knew that if she gave the slightest of tugs he'd free her.

"No apology necessary. Gregory and I are like the Hatfields and the McCoys. We've been sniping at each other for so long I don't think either of us remembers how or why the feud began." She gave him a conciliatory smile. "You and Leslie Faye must have had a lengthy telephone conversation. She's over there working on a truce, and you're over here . . ."

"Uh-uh." His thumb feathered across the fragile skin of her wrist in a circular motion. "There are no ulterior motives for my being here."

She took a shallow breath. He's only touching your wrist. Don't panic.

"None?" she blurted.

He shook his head. "Word of honor."

His eyes were wide open as though he had nothing to hide. She heard nothing from her inner voice. "I believe you."

Sylas couldn't explain why her believing him was of the utmost importance, but it was. He felt as though he'd broken through the emotional barrier Alana had erected between herself and the rest of the world.

He released her hand, separated a slice from the rest of the pizza and offered it to her, then he helped himself to another piece.

"I set up a desk for you in my office. Close quarters, but with both of us working on the date rape survey I thought sharing an office would be expedient."

"What about people to distribute and compile it?" Back on familiar ground, work, Alana began to relax.

"There's a small company in Houston that specializes in that type of work. Should I contact them?"

"It would give us more time to work on the questions you'll be asking the jurors."

She looked directly at him to see if he balked at her coaching him; most attorneys became defensive on this point.

Sylas nodded. "I'm willing to learn your technique, with one stipulation."

"What's that?"

"No cue cards while I'm actually conducting voir dire." He grinned.

"No cue cards, only notes to keep you posted on how the jurors are reacting to each other's replies to your questions."

"What if the judge doesn't allow you at the bar?"

Alana was well aware of the courtroom protocol that restricted anyone other than attorneys from the table inside the courtroom railing. "The judge has a crowded docket. He wants speed and efficiency as much as we do. You'll have to approach the bench and convince him my being next to you is in the court's best interest."

"Put in that light, I don't think a judge will object."

"They rarely do." Alana wiped her hands on her napkin and gave a satiated sigh. "That was superb. My compliments to the chef and the deliveryman. Thanks."

"My pleasure." He closed the lid on the remainder of the pizza, picked up the box and crossed to the refrigerator. "Great for leftovers, too."

"What are you grinning from ear to ear about?"

"Eating cold pizza for breakfast. My father insisted on my leaving the kitchen to do it so I wouldn't spoil his breakfast."

Chuckling, Alana picked up the glasses and moved to the sink. She dampened a cloth to wipe the table. "And here I thought I was the only person with a cast-iron stomach."

"You?" He glanced at her to see if she was pulling his leg. She was bent over the table, scrubbing it in a circular motion. Her backside rotated like that of a puppy wagging its tail. Cute, he thought, enjoying the view. "Why can't I get a mental picture of you eating leftovers from dinner, for breakfast?"

Looking over her shoulder, she replied, "Come to think of it, I usually have a bowl of bran flakes. Oh well, I guess with age comes wisdom, huh?"

"Wisdom or a king-size bottle of antacid on the nightstand."

His eyes followed her when she moved back to the sink. He noticed her easy grace, her dark shiny hair unbound and swaying across her shoulders and her bare feet . . . with pink polish on her toenails!

"Care to walk off some calories?" he suggested. "There's a full moon and a southerly breeze."

A romantic moonlit stroll along the beach? she mused. A hunger unrelated to food curled in the pit of her stomach.

Sylas moved a couple of paces closer to her. The expression on his face communicated an interest in her that had nothing to do with court cases or courtroom procedures.

"No, thanks. I have work to do." Her hands wrung the dishcloth and she draped it over the spigot. "You go right ahead, though."

Shrugging, Sylas shoved his hands in his pockets to keep them from framing her face while he used his powers of persuasion to change her mind. "Unattached and not taking any chances on changing the status quo."

"That sums up my case," she replied, reluctant to take her eyes off the wet dishcloth.

Although she stood a yard away from him she could feel his magnetism tugging at her. She'd read psychological studies that promoted the theory that certain people have a golden aura around them. Sylas had to be one of the golden people.

He glanced at his watch, dreading the thought of going back to his empty condo. "There's a good movie on cable television in a few minutes."

"I shouldn't. Really, I have two volumes you gave me to read before we start working on the survey. You don't want me to be unprepared, do you?"

Sylas thought for a moment. He rubbed his hand across his jaw. "Yeah. I do."

"But you wouldn't respect me in the morning, would you?" Her face turned crimson when she realized the sexual connotation he could place on her innocent remark. "I mean...I didn't say that to be provocative."

Laughing at the absurdity of his misinterpreting what she meant, Sylas turned toward the door.

"Thanks for the dinner company. Next time I'll ask before I arrive on your doorstep." He sketched her a small salute and opened the door. "Lock it. G'night, Alana."

She heard the door quietly click shut and she should have given a heartfelt sigh of relief. She did sigh, but not for the right reason.

"The survey is in three parts, ten questions in each," Alana said, handing a rough draft to Leslie Faye and Sylas.

Her eyes felt scratchy from lack of sleep. To keep from thinking about moonlit strolls and Sylas Kincaid, she'd worked on this survey until she'd fallen asleep with her notepad and pencil on her lap.

Leslie Faye's insisting she accompany Alana to the office had come as a welcome surprise. Alana wanted her friend to take an active part in jury selection. But she noticed Leslie Faye had situated her chair to get an unrestricted view of the hallway and began to wonder if she wanted to work on her case or work on her ex-husband.

"Phase one gives us general information about the person being surveyed. Age, sex, job, family's jobs, hours spent watching television, subscriptions to newspapers and magazines and so forth. This gives us an idea of what might influence the person's answers on the survey. Any questions?"

Sylas glanced through the pages to keep his eyes off Alana. Thoughts of her had bothered him long past midnight. He'd decided she was a lady who'd like to have her life arranged in neat columns that tallied up to a tidy, predictable answer. From all outward appearances, she'd accomplished that goal.

But Sylas felt confident she'd left out some important numbers that affected the final answer. In her case two and two didn't make four. Mathematics hadn't been his best subject in school, but Alana Benton had become an equation he wanted to solve. She was a challenge to him.

"Phase two determines general attitudes toward the government and courtroom proceedings. Basically, we want to know if the panel starts the selection process predisposed in favor of the prosecution. Do they think anyone one brought to trial must be guilty."

"What about innocent until proved guilty?" Leslie Faye asked. "On television that's always brought out."

"Fiction, my dear," Alana replied dryly. "Generally, more than half of the jurors think a defendant wouldn't be brought to trial unless the prosecuting attorney has a solid case against him or her. What we need to find out is if Avery's give-every-dog-his-day-in-court reputation is working for or against him. If he's taking every case to trial, from armed robbery to jaywalking, the taxpayers may think he's wasting their money. The public wants law and order, but they always have a keen eye on their pocketbooks."

Two pages ahead of her, Sylas said, "And phase three relates to Leslie Faye's case?"

Alana nodded. "Most of these questions deal with the myths surrounding rape in general, and date rape in particular."

She noticed Sylas shift in his chair and glance around the room. He appeared decidedly uncomfortable. "Do either of you have a problem with this part of the survey?"

"I'm glad I'm not the one asking the questions," Leslie Faye replied honestly.

"Then we'll have to work on that problem. You have to be able to look a juror in the eye and convince him that you struck Ed Morgan because—"

"You were physically afraid of him," Sylas interjected.

Alana sent Sylas a dirty look. "Because you knew he was about to attempt to rape you. We'll work together on the questions you'll be asking the potential jurors."

"Me?" Leslie Faye's small hand flew to her neckline. "*I* have to ask them questions?"

Sylas reached across his desk and patted Leslie Faye's other hand to reassure her that everything would be okay.

"Yes," Alana replied firmly. "Both you and Sylas will ask questions to establish a rapport with the jurors. That makes you a person instead of just a defendant, and it makes Sylas someone who creates an environment in which the potential jurors feel it's acceptable to admit to their biases."

"I don't know, Alana," Leslie Faye fretted. Her fingers nervously pleated the fullness of her skirt. "I'm going to be so scared my knees will be knocking together."

"That's okay. Let those prospective jurors know that you're frightened. They can relate to that emotion. At some point in their lives they've been scared, too. But it's absolutely imperative that you make them aware that you have the backbone to stand up to a man twice your size rather than allowing him to sexually abuse you. The jurors will be asking themselves, did you strike him in self-defense? Or did you strike him because hell hath no fury like a woman scorned, which is Ed Morgan's version of what happened? Your directly asking questions shows that you have the grit to strike a blow to save your honor. You hit him in self-defense!"

Leslie Faye's blue eyes rounded in appeal to Sylas for intervention on her behalf.

"Maybe we could think of another tactic," Sylas suggested. "Maybe instead of Leslie Faye directing questions, I could..."

Alana raised her hand to stop him. "No. If she sits in the courtroom like a bump on a log, they'll never believe she had the guts to defend herself. They'll believe Ed Morgan's story."

"Or they'll think she had to be pushed into a corner before she'd use physical force," Sylas argued.

"Weak submissiveness might appeal to the men chosen to serve on the jury, but it won't fool the women for a second." She turned toward Leslie Faye. "Your physical stature is a plus. You're small. You're attractive. Without your opening your mouth, the potential jurors will instinctively know you aren't a violent maniac. What you have to do is convince them that knowing the physical odds were against you, you weren't going to be victimized."

Sylas rose from his chair and came around the corner of his desk to stand beside Leslie Faye. His hand rested on her shoulder to calm her.

"We're getting ahead of ourselves," he said. "Let's get the tabulated results of the survey, then we'll plan our courtroom strategy."

Irritated by the alliance formed against her, Alana asked, "Do either of you two have any problems with the survey?"

"No," they chorused.

Alana tapped the bottom edge of the papers on
Kincaid's desk and fastened them with a paper clip.
She could relate to Leslie Faye's emotional response.
Of course she was extremely apprehensive. But Alana
had expected Sylas, a fellow professional, to back her
decision. Before she could convince their client, she
thought, she'd have to work on Kincaid. She said,
"Then if you'll excuse me, I'll take these out to Carmela to be typed."

"Is there anything else you need me for today? If
not, I've got a shipment of purses to unpack at the
store."

Alana waited at the door for Leslie Faye. Her dark
eyes snapped with impatience as Kincaid murmured
reassurances to her friend. He treated her as though
she might collapse into a heap at any moment. And
Leslie Faye responded accordingly by removing a
hankie from her purse to dab at her eyes.

Alana rolled the papers in her hands into a tight coil
as she braced herself to keep from brushing Kincaid
aside and putting her arm around Leslie Faye.

She reminded herself that sympathy alone wouldn't
get Leslie Faye a verdict of not guilty from the jurors.

As Sylas walked Leslie Faye to the door, he saw the
icy look Alana gave him. What did she think he should
do? he wondered in exasperation. His patience with
her was stretching as thin as the smile he gave her. He
closed his office door behind the two women with just
the hint of a bang.

Alone with Alana in the corridor, Leslie Faye said,
"You're mad at me."

"No." Alana didn't want to discuss the problem
until she'd had her say with Kincaid. He was the one

who was pampering Leslie Faye. It was *his* attitude that needed justification, not his client's.

"Disappointed?"

"No."

"What then? Don't clam up and make me play Twenty Questions."

"Okay." Alana pushed the door open and walked outside toward Leslie Faye's car. She rapped the rolled papers against the palm of her hand. "You're confused about the roles in this drama. I'm not the villain and you're not the trembling virgin tied to the railroad tracks."

Leslie Faye grinned, quickly bouncing back to her usual cheerfulness now that she was out of the law office. "I know that. Ed's the villain."

"Not in the courtroom," she corrected. She tapped the papers against Leslie Faye's shoulder. "You're the defendant—the person the jurors may see in the role of the villain. Ed Morgan is the victim."

"He's the virgin tied to the tracks? Not likely," she replied drolly. "The jurors will never believe that story."

"His scar, not to mention the police reports, support his story. You have to realize that the jurors are programmed to believe anything the prosecuting attorney and the judge tell them to believe. You and Sylas have to convince the jurors and the judge who the real villain is."

"I don't even want to go on the witness stand! The thought of Avery cross-examining me, digging into the intimate details of my love life . . . well . . . it's enough to make me want to throw myself on the mercy of the court and plead guilty!"

Alana knew what she was asking was difficult for Leslie Faye. Her friend had no idea how much Alana's heart went out to her, but she had to sever her own emotional ties to the case and handle it objectively, which was difficult. Damn difficult.

She wanted to grab Leslie Faye's hand and run, and run, and run, until there wasn't a chance of anyone hurting either of them. She'd run away once, and she'd thought she'd escaped from her past. But Leslie Faye had brought her flight path into a full circle. She was right back where she'd started. Only now it was worse than when she'd run away. She had to deal with Leslie Faye's pain as well as her own.

Alana watched Leslie Faye shake her head, rejecting the idea of asking questions of the jurors.

"Can we talk about this later?" Leslie Faye asked. "Maybe Sylas can come up with an alternative plan."

"Yeah. Sure." Alana relented, silently cursing Sylas Kincaid. "I'll see you later."

She watched Leslie Faye's car until it disappeared from sight, planning exactly what she'd say to Sylas Kincaid, then turned and strode back into the building. Deciding she wanted to keep their conversation private, she closed the door behind her as she stepped into his office.

"Mr. Kincaid," she began, addressing him formally, her voice deceptively calm, "you and I need to discuss several issues."

When she entered the room, Sylas had risen from where he was sitting on the corner of his desk. He eased back down. She'd taken the words right out of his mouth. "We certainly do, Ms. Benton."

"Are you aware that pampering Leslie Faye invites her tears?"

"Compassion, Ms. Benton. Something in short supply around here."

Inwardly Alana flinched; outwardly she bristled. "If you think I'm hard-hearted, you wait until the prosecuting attorney starts making mincemeat out of your client. While you're compassionately patting her shoulder and she's weeping buckets of tears, the jury will find her guilty as charged and send her straight to the nearest jail!"

"We aren't in the courtroom yet."

"Ah, yes, the courtroom. Tell me, counselor, how do you plan on defending your teary-eyed client when you can't squeeze the words *attempted rape* through your lips because you don't want to offend Leslie Faye's virgin ears?"

"I seem to recall discussing rape with you yesterday," he pointed out.

"But never in front of Leslie Faye."

"When I'm in the courtroom, I'll say whatever needs to be said."

"Oh, right. You'll manage," she scoffed. "Don't kid yourself. You'll wince every time you pronounce the word *rape*, and the jury will be watching you. And do you know what they'll automatically assume?"

Not waiting for a reply, she paced in front of him as she answered. "They'll assume all their beliefs about rape are true. They'll take one look at Leslie Faye and think...hmm, no bruises, no scars, no hospital reports. She must have been asking for it. She must have teased the poor man until he lost control. Well, we can't blame Ed Morgan, now, can we? Look at her. Those must be tears of remorse for attacking Mr. Morgan."

A red stain crept from beneath Sylas's collar as he strained to be patient until Alana had had her say. His lips barely moved as he asked, "Are you finished?"

"No. I'm not. I've only begun!" Hands on her hips, she lowered her voice to keep from shouting. "Henceforth, I expect you to conduct yourself in a professional manner. You may be the expert on date rape, but I'm the expert on what's going to be in the minds of the jurors. You'd do well to take my advice rather than compassionately siding with the client."

"Are you finished?"

"Until you pull another boner, yes."

Sylas rose to his full height, unbuttoned his jacket and strode toward her. Ms. Benton needed to learn a few home truths about him and about herself. And he was the best man to deliver them.

Chapter Seven

Compassion is not a foul four-letter word, Ms. Benton. Rape is," he said through tightly clenched teeth. "It's not only a violent act against women, it's an insult to every decent man. Don't flaunt the word *professionalism* in front of me! I've read court case after court case where women who testified at the trial of the rapist were verbally raped by his lawyer. You're going to tell me that's professionalism?"

Alana backed away from his ferocity. His piercing gray eyes were as hard as agates. A muscle at the side of his jaw throbbed, marking his effort to contain his anger. She realized he'd fulfilled her first impression of him—Sylas Kincaid was a man who'd fight dirty when necessary. He'd taken her byword, professionalism, and flung it in her face!

"When I read of those men, it sickens me to think that I hold the same law degree they do," he said, replying to his own question as he advanced another step. He pointed at Alana as though his finger were a loaded weapon. "Ms. Benton, if that's the kind of attorney it takes to defend Leslie Faye, you can find yourself another one, a callous son of a bitch who can casually bandy the word *rape* in front of the victim without feeling an ounce of compassion for her. I'm obviously not the best man for the job."

"You can't withdraw from the case." All hell would break loose if he did. Leslie Faye would throw a conniption fit, and Gregory would want to string up Alana on the nearest oak tree. "Can't you take a little constructive criticism?"

"I can. Can you?"

His question hung between them for several seconds. Their eyes locked in a grim battle. As the brittle color of his eyes softened to a warm gray, she contemplated how she would have felt if she'd filed charges against Tom Lane and Sylas had been her attorney. She'd have wanted the compassion he'd shown Leslie Faye.

The stark reality of realizing she wanted his compassion this very minute hit her squarely between the eyes, making her break eye contact. She wanted him to care about what had happened to her!

"Ever heard of an oystacuda?" Sylas asked in a less harsh tone. She'd infuriated him, but when he'd seen the pain-filled shadows in her soulful eyes the sharp edge of his anger had been dulled. "It's a mythological cross between an oyster and a barracuda. One minute it closes up tighter than an oyster, and the next it attacks without provocation."

"There is no such beast in mythology," she disclaimed, much preferring anger to the revelation that she cared about his opinion of her. Dammit, she had every right to be angry with him! She wouldn't let his whimsical sense of humor pierce her tough hide! She wouldn't let him deflect her barbed derision by comparing her to an imaginary creature!

To conceal the smile brought on by a mental image of an aluminum-plated oyster with fins, tail and teeth, she started to duck her head.

Sylas crooked his forefinger at the knuckle and stayed her chin from dropping to her chest.

"Careful," he warned, openly smiling at her. "Your shell might crack if you smiled."

She batted at his hand; he caught her wrist. Her fingers doubled into a tight fist; he brought it to the side of his face.

"I won't let you crawl into a shell and hide," he said. "You may not want me to see the feminine woman—the one who hides beneath a business suit and skins her hair back from her face—as being attractive, but I do."

His backhanded compliment caused color to flood her cheeks. Her eyes skittered from the front of his pale blue shirt to first one side of the office, then the other. She felt her heartbeat accelerate. She couldn't look at him. He'd see the tumult he caused by his gentle touch.

He was too damn close for comfort!

"Damn you, Sylas Kincaid! I choose not to be attractive to men! That only causes problems I can avoid!"

His thumb pried her fingers apart until they rested along his jaw.

"You are an attractive woman, like it or not. Those No Trespassing signs you've posted around you make a man want to detour around them, to search through the oyster bed, fending off the barracuda to discover the treasure buried deep in your heart.''

What he'd said had the same effect on her as prying an oyster shell apart. Her tense muscles relaxed as she felt his hand touch her back, drawing her closer and closer to him. He completely disarmed the barracuda of her will to use her fins to flee or her teeth to bite.

''Those passionate outbursts of yours are like pearls—long-hidden and extremely valuable for their rarity. You want me to believe you're coldhearted, without compassion, a woman devoid of emotion, but you aren't. You wouldn't be here for Leslie Faye if you were.''

Her brown eyes met and held his gray eyes.

She was so close she could feel the smooth texture of his jaw, the leather of his shoe against her instep. And yet the compelling look in his eyes was what held her against him.

''I don't want us involved in a sexual relationship,'' she blurted. She nervously licked her dry bottom lip. ''Passion complicates things. It muddles them.''

''Maybe. Maybe not.''

His eyes dropped to the glistening moist trail the tip of her tongue had left on her lipstick. He wanted to kiss her. His eyes moved back to hers. Silently he communicated his desire.

He felt her tremble in his arms. Did she tremble from awareness of him as a man? Or was she afraid to kiss him?

Lethargically he lowered his mouth toward hers to find the answer to his questions.

His voice was soft, husky as he said, "Admitting you're an attractive female and I'm a male attracted to you should clarify our positions instead of muddle them."

Push him away, her defense mechanisms silently cautioned.

Her hand slid from the side of his face to his chest. She stood on tiptoe. He made her feel feminine, desirable. She wanted to feel his lips against hers. She could almost taste the joyous bubbles of laughter on his lips that were the essence of him. She felt his warm breath against her upturned face.

Shove him away! the incessant voice shrieked. Shove him away from you!

Automatically, Alana responded to the warning. She'd ignored it once with Tom Lane and she'd keenly regretted the consequences. Her fingers pressed against the hard wall of his chest.

"No! Stop it!"

His hands dropped instantly to his side. He stepped backward, exiting her circle of private space.

She whirled away from him. Her fingers covered her mouth as though he had touched her lips. Her eyes clamped shut.

"I don't think my compliment or my wanting to kiss you warrants having you rudely turn your back on me."

"I'm sorry." Her voice was low, muffled by her hand. She took another step toward the office door. "I don't mean to be rude. I just didn't want you to kiss me."

He didn't believe her. He'd seen the yearning in her eyes. Or was what he thought he saw merely a reflection of his own longing to kiss her?

"I can wait," he mused aloud.

She ventured a glance over her shoulder to see if his eyes were lit with humor. They weren't. His shoulders sagged as though she'd landed a low blow. She hadn't meant to hurt him. His melancholy expression tore at her insides.

Alana twined her fingers together and locked them at her waist. Silently she measured the consequences of kissing him, considered where innocent kisses could lead. Kisses between two consenting adults would lead to further physical intimacies.

She knew she'd panic once they progressed beyond the kissing stage. But maybe, she silently argued, maybe I wouldn't panic. He held me. It had felt good, like a hug. She'd liked being close to him.

But what would happen when the relationship became increasingly intimate? She might be able to control her panic while Sylas held her and kissed her, but a man wasn't content with hugs and kisses. What would happen if he wanted to make love to her? Would she panic then?

Being a Southern gentleman, Sylas wouldn't cross-examine her, but he'd wonder why she panicked.

And if she decided to come clean, to tell him what had happened to her, their relationship would be damaged beyond repair. She didn't know what she wanted, but she knew for certain she didn't want pity from Sylas Kincaid.

No, she silently decided after hastily weighing and measuring the pros and cons of their relationship, it was safer to keep him at arm's length.

"It'll be a long wait, Sylas. Don't you see? It's not you. It's me. I'm not willing to take the consequences for falling in love with you."

She snapped her mouth shut to keep from saying too much. Without risking a backward glance, she marched out of his office.

Sylas rocked back on his heels, then forward to the balls of his feet. He wanted to chase after her, but his gut instincts glued his feet to the floor. While he'd refrained from going to her, from wrapping his arms around her, she'd mentally taken a quantum leap into the future, from one kiss to falling in love.

He ruffled his fingers through his hair as he moved to his desk chair.

He felt like a man arrested for a crime he hadn't committed, who'd been uninformed of the charges, and who'd be appearing in a kangaroo court without benefit of council. Alana was his judge and jury. She'd decided, without caring if he was innocent or guilty, that because he was a man, he must be guilty.

Of what? he wondered, not knowing what her thoughts had been. Why was she unwilling to become emotionally involved with him?

His eyes focused on the door that she'd quietly closed behind her as she left him.

Unable to find a reason for her rejection, he traced their disagreement back to the point where it had originated. She'd been angry because he'd politely skirted around the word *rape* in Leslie Faye's presence. Alana had seen that as a major flaw that she immediately sought to remedy. Was she right? Did he flinch?

"Attempted rape," he murmured, pretending Leslie Faye sat in the chair across from him. "Rape."

He felt his skin tighten across his cheeks; his lips straightened into a grimace. Subconsciously, he must have been avoiding verbalizing the reason for Leslie Faye's assault on Ed Morgan.

Why? he wondered.

Several of the divorce cases he'd handled dealt with the unpleasant side of life: nonsupport, adultery, wife abuse. He didn't have a reflexive facial reaction to those tough topics.

Could it be that as a man he felt defensive? Did he identify with Ed Morgan? Had there been dates where he'd persuasively coerced a woman into his bed? Not physically, of course, but verbally perhaps.

He shook his head. He didn't believe he had ever pressured a woman to have sex with him.

He'd made love with Kate, but their lovemaking had seemed natural. They'd both watched television, gone to the movies, read the ads in magazines, and they'd been curious about each other. Over a span of several years, kissing had led to light petting, heavy petting and frustration for both of them. The first time, before he'd left the ranch to go to college, when he'd been certain she'd be marrying him, he'd felt far more nervous and awkward than Kate had seemed.

Since Kate had met and married another man, he'd had brief relationships with other women. Early on, he had realized sex without love, without caring what happened to the woman the next day, left him with a hollow feeling. In fact, now that he'd begun to analyze his sex life, he realized that he was often the one who said no to an invitation into a woman's bedroom.

He liked women, but Kate had spoiled him for meaningless relationships. Even as badly as he'd wanted to kiss Alana, he'd stopped the minute she said no.

Whatever character flaw Alana had seen in him, whatever her reasons were for rejecting him, it wasn't because he fit into the same category as Ed Morgan!

He'd have to find a way to restrain his natural reaction to a distasteful situation. A juror might react unfavorably, misinterpret his body language. He would unwittingly damage Leslie Faye's case.

In future consultations, he resolved, he would have to make a concerted effort to say the phrase *attempted rape* in Leslie Faye's presence, while maintaining a poker face.

He drummed his fingers on his desk, wishing he could replay the confrontation with Alana. He wanted to edit in how he should have replied to her accusations.

The last thing she'd said before vanishing from his office stuck out in his mind. She wasn't willing to take the consequences for falling in love with him. Was she flattering his ego, letting him down gently? Or did she really mean that he wouldn't like the consequences of falling in love with her?

Either way, she'd warned him.

What he had to decide was whether or not to heed her warning. That only took a fraction of a second. He'd take the risk. Anything worth having was worth the risk.

Alana, coming out of her shell and caring for him, would definitely be worthy of taking a risk.

"Read the information on the back of the photograph and tell me if you'd allow this man to be on Leslie Faye's jury."

Alana's ploy to get his eyes off her while she worked at the desk he'd provided in his office failed. Sylas continued to lean back in his chair. His long legs bridged the distance between chair and desk. His feet were crossed at the ankles. His hands were folded on his chest, his thumbs twiddling.

"That shade of blue becomes you," he said, before picking up the picture and scanning the facts neatly printed on the back of it. He turned the picture over. "Is there something hidden in the picture that makes this man unacceptable?"

"I took this picture yesterday afternoon near here." She wanted him to know their encounter hadn't prevented her from getting on with her job. It had, but she would hide that fact if it killed her. When she had the roll of film developed, she'd been dismayed to discover, in indisputable plain black-and-white, that she'd photographed men who physically resembled Sylas. The picture she'd handed him was one of the few exceptions. "Look for clues that might indicate his preconceived ideas about women and sex."

"Western-cut suit?" he guessed, unsure how the way a man dressed reflected his prejudices.

"See his stance? Thumbs tucked under his belt right above his pockets, fingers pointing downward, his hips thrust forward. Have you been to a singles bar?"

Sylas grinned. "No, but if that's an invitation, I accept. What time should I pick you up?"

Alana folded her arms across her waist and stepped back from the desk. Pretending to ignore his comment, she raised one hand to her bottom lip and pinched it. "That man's pose is a carbon copy of the sexy bad guy's stance in a B-grade Western film. Everything about him, from the cut of his clothes to his boots, shouts, 'Hey, I'm a tough hombre. I'm dangerous for any and all women.' See what I mean?"

He noticed how she hugged herself. His smile broadened. Maybe the books on body language made sense. He glanced at the step-by-step list he'd made on a legal pad. Maybe the way to break through her shell was to answer her body signals with opposite signals of his own. What he said aloud was of little importance.

"C'mon, Alana. The guy is at least fifty, balding, and probably hasn't had a lurid thought in decades."

"In the surveys you gave me, did age influence how men responded to the questions?"

"No." He nonchalantly picked up the picture and crossed to stand beside Alana. "Are there clues in the fictitious information you compiled on the back of the picture?"

While he waited for her response, he let his eyes do more talking than his mouth. His eyes narrowed as they dropped from her stiff jawline, lingered on the whiteness of her throat, on the thrust of her breasts and the slimness of her waist. He touched his tongue to his lips.

Loudly, Alana cleared her throat. Was it her imagination or were the golden flecks in his eyes flaring like tiny embers sparking to life? Weren't his eyes bolder than they'd been previously? What the heck did he think he was doing? Reflexively her hands smoothed the side seams of her suit skirt. Damn his eyes if they didn't follow her hands!

"Care to fill me in on exactly what you think you're doing?" she asked, her voice icy.

"Practicing."

"Practicing what?"

"Flattering you with my body language." In hitch-hiker fashion, he pointed his thumb toward the books she'd given him. He raised his eyes and gave her a slow, sexy wink. "It seems to work."

She crossed her arms. "What does this mean?"

"Well," he drawled, stringing out the sounds, "the classical interpretation is that you're rejecting my subtle advances. But then again, it might mean that you're frustrated. That you're locked inside of yourself and you're begging to be set free."

Alana groaned and dropped her arms. "I've created Frankenstein's monster!"

Chuckling, Sylas mimicked the male pose they'd been discussing, as his elbow brushed against her forearm. "Are you into science fiction?"

"I'm into getting your mind back on the case," she primly replied. He was close enough for her to smell his after-shave. It probably had some tacky name, she mused, guaranteed to draw females into his clutches.

"Attempted rape. Notice how I can say it with a deadpan face? The jurors will never know I find the concept of a man forcing himself on a woman repulsive. Other than your accusation that I'm too compassionate, which I don't care to change, is there anything else that bothers you?"

You, she wanted to reply, but managed to keep the word behind tightly compressed lips. The dream she'd had last night had featured him in the starring role, only he hadn't forced her to make love with him. She'd been anxious to comply with his smallest wish.

A complete reversal of her traditional nightmare.

Get your mind off his fragrance and how it would feel to be in his arms, she coached. Get back to the business at hand!

"There's a stack of pictures on my desk." She sidestepped around him. "I'll get them. I photographed people who sent clear messages and people who were difficult to decipher, and then shuffled the prints in a random order. Look at them. Make notes. The ones who don't overtly give you clues are the type of people you'll have to direct questions to in the courtroom.''

She handed him the pictures, then glanced at her watch. She'd made arrangements to meet Leslie Faye at the Baybrook Mall in Clear Lake City.

''This afternoon we'd better go shopping for you. Just as the potential jurors' clothing sends messages to you, your clothing transmits messages about you to them, too.''

''What sort of message would they receive if I was in the courtroom today?''

She gave him a thorough once-over. He'd implied she was an oystacuda. She was tempted to return his backhanded compliment by calling him a clotheshorse.

''Your suit, shirt and tie cost more than the average jurors' take-home pay each month. They expect you to dress like a professional, but they resent your higher income. An attorney who wears expensive clothing creates a psychological gap between himself and them. Your image is important.''

''Suits made of sackcloth don't come in my size,'' he teased lightly. ''But I do have some jeans with holes in the knees that I've worn to clean the stables. That should make them feel superior to me and get sympathy for my client.''

Alana grinned. ''Case studies prove that attractive people get away with a lot more than unattractive people. I'd say both you and Leslie Faye have the edge, provided you don't alienate the jurors by overdressing." She took another look at her wristwatch. "I'm supposed to meet Leslie Faye for lunch and a shopping spree. Can we meet outside the south entrance to the Baybrook Mall at one-thirty?"

"It's been a long time since a woman picked out my clothes for me."

The thought of Alana tugging on his jacket sleeve and running her hands along the back of his shoulders brought a wry smile to his lips. She'd have to touch him. This promised to be an interesting encounter, one he planned on fully enjoying.

Chapter Eight

Isn't this gorgeous?'' Leslie Faye asked. She held up a navy-blue chiffon, strapless jumpsuit with a bolero jacket accented in white soutache. She draped it across Alana's front. "It's perfect for you. It'll accent your coloring and those long, long legs of yours. Back at my shop I have a fabulous pair of large button earrings with rhinestones glittering in the centers. They'll make your eyes sparkle like black diamonds. What do you think?"

"I think we've been through every women's shop in the mall," Alana moaned as she collapsed into the first chair she saw. She slipped off one of her high-heeled shoes and massaged her aching foot.

Leslie Faye held the garment out to her. "You promised."

"No. I absolutely, positively refuse to try it on. I promised I'd shop *a little* after we found a couple of appropriate dresses for you. We shopped *a lot!*"

"I kept my end of the bargain. Didn't I buy those atrocious somber-colored dresses with high necks, long sleeves and flared skirts? Believe me, after the trial those monstrosities are going in the back of my closet. Honestly, Alana, I haven't seen Peter Pan collars since the two of us went rummaging through my mother's trunks up in the attic." Undaunted by Alana's silence, she shrugged. "I guess it's better than bold black and white stripes."

Leslie Faye marched around one rack, then turned to another. "I don't want to hurt your feelings, but even...even right after Ed Morgan attacked me, I dressed better than you do. It's a good thing Sylas talked some sense into my head. He said it didn't matter how low my neckline dipped or how short the skirt was that I wore that night." She circled back to where Alana sat. "Are you pouting because I hurt your feelings?"

"I quit pouting in fourth grade. It's my feet that hurt. You've walked them off to the anklebone!"

Alana's plea of fatigue was true, but it also gave her a chance to think about how her incident with Tom Lane had altered the type of clothing she wore. When she left Texas, there had been no one to keep her from donating her college clothes to the Salvation Army. Nor had she had anyone like Sylas to supply her with information on the subject of date rape. She'd had to survive on her own. Gradually over the years her wardrobe had changed from shapeless dark-colored clothing to classic suits in brighter colors.

"I'm only trying to help you spiff up your wardrobe."

"The night I arrived you said I looked good in a flour sack." Alana sighed, crossed her legs the other way and began massaging her left foot. "My clothes are practical and serviceable."

"Spinsterish!" Leslie Faye snorted delicately. "Your clothes should have been pitched five years ago. I can remember when I used to want to grow five inches so I could borrow your clothes. Now, I wouldn't give them away to the Goodwill Store. They'd refuse shipment."

Alana held up the bag that contained her purchases. "I bought a couple of blouses."

"White. High-collared. Plain as the nose on my grandmother's face."

"And a silk dress. You picked it out, so don't you dare gripe about it." Not that I'll wear it, Alana silently added. Where did Leslie Faye think she'd wear a scoop-necked, sleeveless dress made up in a jungle print? To the St. Louis Zoo?

"It looks fantastic on you. One more outfit, then I'll figure you've kept your side of the bargain." She dropped the jumpsuit in Alana's lap. "Do you try this on or do we head for Macy's?"

"That's made of chiffon."

"So?"

"It clings."

"Yeah." Leslie Faye grinned. "To all the right places. It'll turn you into a chic woman instead of a dried-up stick. Do I put it back?"

"Watch my shoes. I don't think my feet will fit back into them," she replied none too graciously. She levered herself to her feet when a brilliant idea struck her. "You're right. I love this outfit. It's my size, isn't it?"

"It's a ten. You might need a smaller size."

Alana limped to the mirror, held the garment up to her shoulders to check the length, stretched the elastic at the waist and said, "It'll fit. Trust me."

"You don't want to try it on?"

"Nope. What I want to do is squeeze my feet into those shoes, pay for the jumpsuit and start hobbling toward the other end of the mall."

"We can always bring it back if it doesn't fit." Leslie Faye's blue eyes twinkled at the prospect of another excuse to take Alana shopping. "We haven't hit all the stores."

Alana grimaced as her big toe pinched against her second toe. She sympathized with Cinderella's wicked stepsisters, the ones who couldn't get their feet into the glass slipper. There wouldn't be another marathon shopping excursion with Leslie Faye if she could avoid it. And if she couldn't avoid one, she'd wear her running shoes. To hell with the idea that she had to dress up to impress the salesclerk!

"Wait just a minute," Leslie Faye said with a gasp. "Look over there on the back wall. Isn't that eye-catching?"

Alana opened her purse and plopped her sunglasses on her nose. "I'm going to pay for this."

"But it would be perfect for you to wear to the cocktail party."

"I'm not going to a cocktail party." Alana gingerly rose to her feet. "Let's go."

"Hasn't Sylas invited you to the little political get-together at the Galvez? Gregory and I are going, and I know Sylas is planning to go as well."

"No."

"You will go with him when he invites you, won't you?"

"No." Alana adjusted her sunglasses. "We have a strictly business relationship."

Leslie Faye moaned aloud. "Remember that card game we used to play? Old Maid? That's going to be you."

"Please. I prefer to think of myself as a—"

"Swinging single?" Leslie Faye's blond eyebrows rose until they almost met her hairline.

"As a career woman. Amen. Closed subject."

Alana felt as though her anklebone was connected to her hipbone as she trudged toward a salesclerk. Merciful God, she silently prayed, please let her think I'm related to somebody famous so she'll ring this up fast.

"Thank you," Alana muttered when the young woman took the hanger off her finger. "It's cash."

"Alana, I want to try this on." Leslie Faye held up a sequined dress that made Alana glad she had her sunglasses on. "I know how you hate to be late for an appointment. Why don't you go on ahead? Leave your packages with the salesclerk and I'll take them back to the condo for you."

"Thanks." Alana gave her friend a wave and headed for the exit.

Each and every step Alana took made her want to remove her shoes again. Only the thought of dozens of shoppers giving her a second look kept them on her feet. As she tottered by a shoe store she considered stopping to buy a pair of flats. But even if Sylas was long on patience, she prided herself on being punctual.

She arrived at the appointed place just as Sylas jogged from his parked car to the mall entrance. She wiggled her toes in her shoes while admiring his natural athletic grace. A smile lit his face at the exact moment she felt her big toe rise upward.

Sylas lengthened his stride when he saw her face blanch. "Is something wrong?" he called.

"A charley horse in my leg." She limped over to the concrete bench beside the entrance. "It'll pass."

He dropped to one knee in front of her. Pulling her shoe off her foot, he began kneading her calf. "I used to get these when I ran cross-country races back in college. They hurt like the devil."

"You're telling me," she muttered, catching her breath. "I ran a crisscross-the-mall race with Leslie Faye. I thought I was in decent shape until I tried to keep pace with her."

"You're still in shape." With his hands on her legs and his head within inches of her breasts, he considered himself a reliable witness who was willing to give testimony on her physical attributes.

"No flattery. Not while I'm in pain. My defenses are down." She gulped short breaths between sentences.

Sylas grinned up at her. "It's the truth, the whole truth and nothing but the truth."

Gradually the muscle contraction eased. Sylas began stroking from behind her knee to the back of her ankle. "Do you have these often?"

"Once a month, maybe. I should have known better than to point my toes and wiggle them."

His left hand rotated the ball of her foot. His thumb made small circles at the joints of each toe, one by one.

"You're in the wrong business," she said. "You should be a podiatrist."

"And you should drink more milk. Leg cramps are sometimes caused by a calcium deficiency. Have you had lunch?"

"No. Leslie Faye doesn't stop shopping just for food!"

He shoved her shoes in his jacket pockets. "I'll treat you to a milk shake."

Before she realized what he was about to do, he'd got to his feet, with her in his arms.

"I can walk," she protested, twisting in his arms. She'd crawl if necessary.

"Just put your arm around my neck and shut up."

"I'm heavy." Her head turned from side to side. Several people walking to or from their cars were watching her. "Put me down. People are gawking at us."

"Only because you're struggling. They probably think I'm kidnapping you. Unless you want the police here asking questions, you'd better tuck your face against the side of my neck and enjoy the ride."

Sylas liked the feel of her. Silky threads of her dark hair blew across his face as she relaxed against him. Although she wore no perfume, he could smell the fragrance of lightly scented soap. He almost regretted having parked his car so close to the mall entrance. With great reluctance he lowered her to the pavement beside his Mercedes.

"Is your car here?" he asked.

She balanced on her left leg while he opened the door. "I rode with Leslie Faye."

"Good. That'll save us a trip back here."

"Sylas, we have to select a suit for you."

"Not today we don't. You've been working day and night since you arrived. This leg cramp could be stress related." He helped her into his car. "I'm going to take you to a drive-through restaurant. Then I'm going to carry you to the beach, plunk you on a beach blanket and force-feed you, if necessary."

He closed the car door before she could open her mouth. She touched the side of her face that had pressed against his neck. His skin had been warm, pleasant to the touch. He'd carried her without so much as breathing hard.

She stared out the window while he skirted the back of the car, slightly amazed that she'd been completely calm while he held her tightly. In fact, she'd even taken his advice and enjoyed being carried.

Only for a second had her silent alarm system jangled—when he said he'd force her to eat. No man could force her to do anything, not without her screaming her head off.

Her hand drifted across her chest to her stomach. She had to admit she was hungry. He wouldn't have to force her to eat.

"Buckle up." He started the engine and pulled forward through an empty parking space. "What's your favorite burger joint?"

Thirty minutes and half a chocolate milk shake later, Alana stretched out her legs on the beach blanket. She felt secure knowing dozens of vacationers were strolling along the beach. Her face tilted toward the sun, drinking in its rays. She'd ruined her nylons by insisting on walking unassisted across the worn boards, but she couldn't have cared less.

"French fry?" Sylas asked, dangling one over her mouth. "I kept them separate from the hamburgers and shakes."

Alana opened her mouth. "You're never going to let me live down my eating habits, are you?"

"Nope. I like a woman who knows exactly how she wants things arranged. Another?"

"Mmm. I used to love picnics and parties on the beach."

"Salt?"

He held his finger over her mouth, waiting for her tongue to dart out for a granule of salt. Her mouth went dry at the thought of licking the salt off his skin. She was tempted, but shook her head.

"It'll make me thirsty." Thirstier, she corrected silently as she sneaked a peek at the flecks of salt clinging to the corner of his mouth.

She wondered what kissing Sylas would be like. She imagined he'd be gentle. His lips would be closed, barely brushing against hers.

She focused her wayward eyes and thoughts on the horizon where the sea touched the sky. Don't think about kissing Sylas, she chided herself.

Sylas wiped his mouth on a paper napkin. He lay back, then rolled to his side. He liked how her hair drawn back to her nape accentuated her profile, but he felt an urge to unclasp the barrette restricting her hair from blowing free. He wanted to unbutton the top three buttons of her dress to let the breeze kiss her throat.

Who was he kidding? What he really wanted was to thread his fingers through her hair and do his own kissing!

To get his mind off his libidinous thoughts, he asked, "Did Leslie Faye mention the cocktail party Gregory and I have been invited to Friday night?"

"Yeah." Alana lay back with her fingers laced behind her head. The barrette gouged her fingers; she removed it. "She'd like to play matchmaker between the two of us, but I discouraged her."

Bless Leslie Faye, Sylas mused, grinning. She'd paved the way for him to invite Alana as his date. "I'd enjoy taking you."

Alana closed her eyes. She wanted to accept. She couldn't tell if it was the bright yellow light of the sun filtering through her eyelids or caution lights coming from her mind, but it didn't matter. She had to refuse him.

"No, but thanks."

"Because we had a quarrel yesterday?"

He willed her to open those big brown eyes of hers and look at him. She was shutting him out and he disliked it, intensely.

"Is that why you invited me? As a penance for calling me an oystacuda?"

"I invited you because I'd enjoy your company." He shifted closer, bracing his arm on the other side of her shoulder, blocking the sun from her face. "I didn't invite you because of guilt feelings or because Leslie Faye suggested it. I told you yesterday that I'm attracted to you."

When she didn't respond, he asked, "Why are you afraid of falling in love?"

"Who says I'm afraid?" she murmured, unable to answer his question honestly.

"You said you didn't want to kiss me because you didn't want to risk the consequences of falling in love with me. What are the grave consequences that frighten you?''

Alana barely parted her eyelashes and looked up at him. Her fingers curled against the palms of her hands; she could feel her nails making half-moon prints on her skin.

Since her arrival in Houston, she'd begun to realize she hadn't recovered from Tom Lane's assault. She'd thought she had, but now it turned out she'd just buried the incident in her subconscious. Being around Leslie Faye, listening to her, had brought back the pain. And she realized her friend was psychologically recovering far faster than she had.

She attributed some of Leslie Faye's speedy healing to emotional support from Gregory and Sylas. While Alana had blocked her experience from her mind, Leslie Faye had been forced to talk about hers.

Alana had never told anyone what had happened to her or why she steered away from involvement, but she found herself wanting to tell Sylas.

Maybe it was because he was a good listener. Maybe it was because she grown to trust him. Or maybe it was because he knew more about date rape than anyone she'd met. Whatever her reasons, she knew now that she would never completely recover until she talked to someone.

She opened her eyes and stared up at Sylas. He'd learned to say ''attempted rape'' without flinching. How would he react to hearing what had happened to her?

She began by admitting what she'd been the most afraid to think about. ''I'm physically petrified of men.''

Sylas felt the muscles of his shoulders bunch together, but he kept his face open to anything she'd tell him. "Can you tell me why?"

"Remember how I fainted at the airport?"

He nodded.

"It wasn't because I'd been drinking during the flight. Leslie Faye hadn't told me the circumstances that led up to charges being filed against her. I guess the reason I was so hard on you yesterday about your being unable to say 'attempted rape' was because *I* had to force them through my lips. My sophomore year in college I was the victim of date rape."

She looked into his eyes expecting to see pity or disgust. Momentarily his lips tightened, but she could understand his being shocked.

She pushed against his arm, still braced beside her, until he moved it. She sat up, drew her knees against her chest, then wrapped her arms around her legs. She could no longer look at him as she spoke. Her own face was reflected in the dark pupils of his eyes.

"There was this guy in my Western Civilization class I thought was cute. I had a crush on him." Her voice held little inflection as she continued. "We chatted a couple of times walking down the hallway after class. He seemed nice. We both lived in the same dormitory.

"One afternoon I was studying at the library. He arrived and sat down at the same table, only across from me. I could hardly concentrate on my homework. After a while, I packed up my books. He did, too. He invited me to stop to get something to eat."

Her eyes closed as she tried to remember the details. Her arms slid up to her knees. She brushed her forehead against them.

"I can't remember much about what we ate—burgers and fries, I guess. I don't remember what we talked about. I do remember thinking how lucky I was to be with him." Her lips curled downward. She scoffed, "Lucky? Stupid is more accurate.

"We walked back to the dorm hand in hand. I was on cloud nine. On the way, we lingered under an old oak tree. I remember how I felt when he kissed me. The earth seemed to tremble under my feet. Skyrockets burst overhead. I thought everything I'd ever read about falling in love was coming true. When he said he wanted to drop off his books at his room, then we'd drop off mine and go catch a movie, a warning bell rang in my head, but I blithely ignored it. All I thought about was his hugs and kisses and how wonderful it would be to go to the movies with him.

"We got to his room. No one was there but the two of us. Again I heard a warning voice, but I wouldn't listen."

Sylas silently nodded. In the case studies he'd read, the victim often felt uncomfortable, but ignored it.

"The next thing I knew, I was flat on my back with him grabbing at me. I tried to push him off me, to reason with him."

The mental picture in her mind became vivid. Her voice choked until it was a tight whisper. She could feel hot tears scalding the back of her throat.

"I'm not like that. No. No." Mentally she heard the sound of cloth ripping at the seams. She covered her ears. Her legs clenched together as she remembered how she'd felt when his fingers had dug into her upper thighs. "Don't do that. Don't touch me there. You're hurting me. Can't you tell I've never had sex with a man? Please, don't do this!"

A harsh laugh that held no humor pushed through her lips. "Can you believe that I kept my voice down because I didn't want the entire dorm to hear me screaming? I didn't want to embarrass him? I never dreamed going to his room meant he'd think I'd have sex with him. I should have screamed. I know I was screaming inside my head. I should have hit him or scratched him or bitten him. Something. But I didn't. Afterward, I put my clothes on and went to my room.

"While I showered, scrubbing my skin raw to get the scent of him off me, I couldn't believe what had happened to me. I thought about calling the police, but what would I tell them? He hadn't held a knife to my throat or a gun to my head. He hadn't even hit me. I realized they'd never believe me. No one would believe me."

She glanced at Sylas. He looked like a wood carving. Only the muscle along the side of one cheek jerked.

"I was ashamed. Humiliated. I couldn't even share what happened with my best friend, Leslie Faye. I don't think she knew anything was drastically wrong. I made excuses—said I wasn't able to eat or sleep because I was worried about semester exams. Actually, I was scared.

"This guy had his roommate give Leslie Faye my books, but the next day he called me and asked for a date. At first, I was speechless. I couldn't believe he'd forced me to have sex with him and wanted me to go out with him again. I just said, 'No, thank you,' like he was a stranger.

"He called daily. I refused his calls. Finally, when I thought I was going stark raving crazy, I decided to transfer out after the semester. Considering the fact I flunked most of my finals, it's a wonder I could transfer.''

Sylas looped his arm across her shoulders and pulled her close to him, as though he could shelter her from future pain, absorb her present pain.

"I truly thought I'd adjusted, until Leslie Faye told me what happened to her.'' Her arm crept up around Sylas's neck. Her fingers clenched and unclenched on his shirt fabric. His tightly holding her gave her the fortitude to finish. "I hadn't dealt with it at all. I was like an ostrich with its head in the sand. This has happened to other women. It's been in the media, but I couldn't bear to watch it or read about it.''

"Until I gave you stacks of material about date rape,'' Sylas said, his voice hoarse with emotion. "That must have hurt you.''

Alana sniffed. She rubbed her knuckles into her eyes. "I couldn't have read them that first night. It was childish, but I went to bed behind a locked door with the lights on, as though those books were a grown-up version of the bogeyman, as though I wouldn't have been safe if I'd brought them into my room.''

Sylas stroked his hand along the length of her hair and across her back. He felt responsible for part of her pain. What she had told him explained her actions. No wonder she kept a wide circle around her. He felt like kicking himself for kidding her about being an oystacuda. She had good reason to be standoffish, to bare her teeth when a man came too close.

"You're safe, Alana. You're careful. It won't happen again,'' he soothed. Suddenly it occurred to him why she'd drawn up the no-publicity document. She was afraid that the bastard who'd done this to her might be in Galveston. "Was he from Galveston?''

"Uh-uh. North of Houston."

"Did you look to see if his name was in the phone directory?"

"Yeah. If he's in the area, he has an unlisted number."

"He's probably long gone."

"Do you really think so?" She wanted to believe Tom had vanished from the face of the earth. "Do you?"

For her peace of mind, he hoped so. He couldn't pry the man's name out of her, but for her sake he wished he'd run across him . . . with his bare knuckles.

"The slump in the economy caused many people to pull up stakes. Maybe he went to work for a big company and got transferred to Lower Slobovia. But to be safe, you should continue to be careful."

"I am. Too careful. I'm so afraid of my poor judgment in regard to men that I've sentenced myself to solitary confinement." She leaned back in his arms. "You asked me if I'd been lonely. I lied. I can be in an ocean of people, but because I'm scared to death to reach out and touch someone . . . or be touched, I'm constantly lonely."

His eyes locked with hers. He framed her heart-shaped face with his large hands. He looked for dark shadows of fear, but her soulful eyes were bright and clear.

"What can I do to help you?"

"Help me pull my head out of the sand." Her lips curved slightly, but her chin wobbled, spoiling the effect she sought. "Humor me, just once."

"How?" He'd have done anything for her. He felt her tremble with apprehension. "Trust me, Alana."

Her hands shyly feathered across the yoke of his shirt. Her eyes timidly drifted from the warm grayness of his eyes to his lips. Her slender body swayed toward him.

She spoke not a word, but he received the subtle hints she communicated to him.

Chapter Nine

Slow and easy, he mused. He had to be patient. He had to let her set the pace. One hasty move and she'd bolt back inside her shell. Although the weight of responsibility rested on his shoulders, he bore it with confidence. Now that he understood the reasons for her elusiveness, he promised himself his patience would be limitless.

I will never frighten you, he silently pledged.

His lips brushed against hers. He expected her to tense, to pull away as she had when he'd casually touched her. The air she'd trapped inside her chest sighed through her parted lips.

She whispered against his mouth, "I can taste your smile. It lingers here...and here." She lightly kissed the corners of his mouth.

His eyes were open, gray as a rainy day that promised a soft gentle rain to nurture the spring flowers into full bloom. His lips slanted over hers, ever so slightly. One, two, three seconds passed. Slowly, he withdrew.

Her arms cradled his neck; her fingers combed through the fine texture of his hair. Her neck bent as she stared at his shirt where he'd removed his tie and unbuttoned his collar. Whorls of dark hair showed against the pale blue fabric. His tan appeared darker beneath his chest hair.

Sylas brought her completely against him. His hands encircled her waist. Knees, thighs and shoulders touched. Her breasts flattened against his chest. He could feel her nipples harden through the thickness of his cotton shirt.

Alana arched her back. The seductive patterns he sketched across her shoulder blades and spine sent shivers of pleasure cascading through her.

The public setting of the beach and the knowledge that there was no real danger with Sylas gave her the courage to sway her shoulders. Her breasts rubbed against his chest. The sensual friction brought a low groan from the back of her throat.

Sylas concentrated on the sound of the Gulf breaking against the shore, a sea gull squawking overhead, a mother calling to her child, but the small moan of pleasure Alana gave quickened his pulse. Common sense told him he was dangerously close to going beyond comforting her.

"Enough," he whispered unsteadily.

Alana sank back on her heels. Her hands trailed down his arms. She turned her hands palms upward, then raised her fingers to her lips. "How could I have forgotten how good it feels to be kissed?"

"Think about it, Alana." He needed to help her put what had happened into perspective. She had to reckon with her past before she could go on with her future. "You locked the good memories behind the bad ones. What happens between a man and woman who care about each other is beautiful."

Her brow wrinkled as she listened to him.

He picked up her hand and twined their fingers together. "Listen to me, Alana. You've read the case studies and the statistics. It's important that you begin to believe in yourself. You were a victim, just as Leslie was almost a victim. Do you blame her for what happened or do you blame Ed Morgan?"

"Ed Morgan."

"Then show the same clemency for yourself that you've given her. What happened wasn't your fault. You aren't the guilty party."

"Maybe."

"Maybe? Alana, what are you guilty of?"

"I should have known when he wanted me to come into his room that he wanted a payback for buying dinner."

"Think about it, carefully. Did you have money in your purse to pay for what you ate?"

She nodded. "I thought it would be Dutch treat, so I checked how much money I had before I ordered. He insisted on paying the check."

"Ed bought Leslie Faye dinner. Did that entitle him to a payback?"

"No. But even if I'd paid for dinner, I should have known better than to go to his room."

"Why? It was something everybody did, wasn't it? I know they did at my college."

"I should have screamed. Fought." Her free hand formed a fist. "I should have done what Leslie Faye did."

"Alana, you were a safe victim. You didn't want to make a scene, did you?"

"No."

"Do you remember what you were thinking?"

Her eyes closed as she searched her memory. "I thought he'd say we were necking and I panicked. That I was making a big deal out of nothing. I kept telling myself that he'd stop, that he wasn't really going to do it."

"Denial. You've read about it in the case studies. And with denial comes dissociation. It's a mental defense mechanism that helped you survive what was happening."

She looked up at Sylas. "It was like I left my body, like I was standing next to the bed. I kept thinking, 'He's going to hurt her. He's going to hurt her really bad.' But I couldn't stop what was happening to her."

"And afterward, tell me what you felt."

"Anger." Her fingers tightened around Sylas's knuckles. "I was mad as hell at myself for not being in control of the situation. I promised myself I'd never—" her eyes met his "—be in a situation where I wasn't in control."

"You've kept that promise, Alana, but it's had a price. You generalized one specific instance until it affected everything in your life. You put yourself on trial, took the blame and sentenced yourself to existing without any form of love."

He brought her palm to his lips. "Don't you think it's time to pardon yourself?"

"For exemplary behavior?"

"No. For being totally innocent of the crime." He kissed her palm and folded her fingers over it for safekeeping. "To me, you're as innocent as the day you walked into that man's dorm room."

She wanted to believe him. Since she'd read the case studies, she'd already begun to think of herself as a victim. With her hand in his, she said, "I want exactly what Leslie Faye and the other victims want."

"Tell me."

"I want everything in my life to be normal again. I want my dreams and aspirations to be what they were before this happened. I survived, but ten years of my life are gone. I only existed. I want to stop existing and start living. Does that make sense to you?"

"Absolutely."

Her eyes dropped to the sand beside the blanket. And I want him to be a part of this new life, she mused. She admired his integrity, his decency. And finally, she could admit to being physically attracted to him without cringing inside.

Feeling like a toddler about to take her first step, she lifted her head and asked, "Can I change my mind about going to the cocktail party as your date?"

"I'd hoped you would," he answered. The way she looked at him made him feel ten feet tall and invincible. He rose to his feet, pulling her along with him. "We'll go slowly, but I want you to know that I think you're one brave, lovely woman."

She returned his compliment with the highest tribute she could give to a man. "I trust you."

During the remainder of the work week, Alana learned why Gregory and Leslie Faye believed Sylas was the best man to represent Leslie Faye. Sylas had what Alana called the three S's—sincerity, strength and sensitivity. As a bonus, he was a man who could disclose his feelings without feeling uncomfortable. Jurors would be able to open up to Sylas because they'd know, as she herself had discovered, that he wasn't judgmental.

Alana smiled as she sat at her desk watching him writing. As though he felt her eyes on him, he glanced up from his work.

"Working hard or hardly working?" he teased, returning her smile.

"Hardly working."

"Daydreaming?"

"I should plead the Fifth." She uncrossed her legs; her hand cupped the side of her face as she propped her elbow on her desk. She noticed the door wasn't ajar; it was firmly closed, which assured them of privacy. Since their discussion at the beach, she'd felt less inhibited with Sylas. "I won't, though. I was thinking about you."

"Oh?" His smile grew. He glanced down at the open-ended questions he'd been preparing to ask the prospective jurors. What better way to field-test his efforts than by asking the same questions of the expert on the subject? "What kinds of descriptive words would you use to describe the subject of your daydream, say to a friend or relative?"

"You have what I call the three S's of a good defense attorney: strength, sincerity, sensitivity."

Her praise pleased him enormously. She respected him as a professional, but he wanted to know what she thought of him as a man. "Make that four S's and I'll be a happy man."

"What's the fourth?"

"Sexy," he mouthed, pushing aside his papers in favor of devoting his complete attention on Alana.

She put her hand to her ear as though she couldn't read his lips. "What?"

"S-e-x-y," he spelled in his normal tone. "Sexy."

"You are kind of cute."

Sylas groaned. "Poodles are cute."

"Yes, they are," she agreed. She pretended to sort through her papers, but she kept one eye on him.

He studied her for a moment, then stood up and crossed between the two desks.

"Did you want something?" she asked innocently.

"I am not cute," he growled. He tucked a strand of hair behind her ear and whispered something deliciously naughty into it.

Alana blushed. "Here?"

"Here." Sylas pointed to her cheek, her neck, and the hollow beneath the top button of her collar. "Hot, wet kisses."

"Aren't you the one who said no hanky-panky during working hours?" She arched her neck, inviting him to carry through his threat. "You should be over there."

He put one hand on the arm of her chair, swiveled her around and pulled her into his arms. He sat on the corner of her desk with her firmly wedged between his muscular thighs. "Take back what you said about me being cute and I'll get back to work."

"Okay. You aren't cute."

"I'm sexy."

"If you say so," she bantered, loving the feel of his arms around her.

"You say it."

She slipped down the knot on his tie, undid his collar button, then rumpled his hair until one dark lock hung rakishly over his forehead. "Now, you're sexy."

"And now do you want me to go back to my desk and get busy?"

"Uh-uh."

"What do you want?"

She walked her fingers up his shirtsleeves until they met at the back of his collar. "Do what you threatened to do."

"This?" His breath, warm, and minty, fluttered over her cheeks as his lips grazed them. "This?"

"Don't stop," she said, when his mouth reached the prim collar of her blouse. He unbuttoned the top two buttons with great agility. "You've had plenty of practice doing that, haven't you?"

He tongued the delicate hollow of her throat before replying, "Hundreds of times. Maybe more."

Her fingers nipped the short hair at his nape. "Wrong answer, counselor."

"In my mind, love. Your buttons. Your blouse. I've been doing nothing but fantasizing about kissing you for the past three days, while you were working."

She smoothed the place she'd tugged. "I've been fantasizing about you, too."

She'd caught him watching her; he'd caught her watching him. The tension between them had escalated as the glances had become longer, hotter, hungrier. Not quite ready to deal with these new emotions until now, she'd quickly glanced in another direction. Respecting her indecisiveness, he'd waited and waited and waited.

Anticipation and excitement built inside of Alana. She knew he'd been patient with her. Figuratively, he'd taken several steps back to give her time to think about him. She'd ended his grace period by not looking away a few minutes earlier.

Her thumb touched his bottom lip, hard. The serrated edges of his front teeth raked across her fingernail.

Her gesture wasn't written up in the books he'd read about body language, but intuitively he understood what she wanted of him. She wanted to be kissed, not gently, but with passion.

His eyes were empty of humor as they met hers; they burned with the desire and passion he'd held in check. He broke eye contact as his mouth slanted over hers, taking full possession, kissing her hard. His lips changed direction as his tongue roved across her lips, seeking and gaining entrance. Boldly he thrust inside, coaxing the tip of her tongue to follow his with long velvet rasps.

"Yes," he crooned softly when she obliged him. He wanted to be aggressive. "Yes. I like that. Kiss me the way you want to be kissed."

Her breasts moved against his chest. His hands edged toward her ribs. His thumb caressed the underside of her breasts. He heard her gasp, which gave him the impetus to cup one breast in his supple hand as he shifted her to the crook of his right arm. He circled her budding nipple through her cotton blouse and lacy bra.

"I'd dreamed of kissing you here, too," he whispered. He strung a hot, wet line of kisses and nibbles down the V of her opened blouse. Momentarily, he felt her hand flutter against his neck. He stopped. "We won't go beyond what feels good to you, Alana," he promised.

Bemused by the tingling sensation coursing through her, she barely heard what he'd said. She was intent on feeling the texture of his mouth against her skin.

Through her clothing she could feel the heated moisture of his breath.

It felt good.

Speechless, she encouraged him by arching her breast toward him. His mouth completely encircled her nipple. A sharp ache centered between her tightly clenched thighs. Her knees threatened to buckle beneath his fiery onslaught. Fairly dizzy from the burst of sensations coursing through her, she clasped his shoulders, digging her fingers into his shirt as she struggled to maintain her balance.

Heavenly, she mused, unable to string her thoughts together into more than one-word descriptions of how he made her feel. Womanly. Fragile. Desirable.

She wished the barrier between his mouth and her skin would magically disappear.

It did, but not by sorcery.

His nimble fingers unbuttoned her blouse and unclipped the front clasp of her bra. For several pulse beats he marveled at the translucent fineness of her skin, the upward thrust of her breast, the rosy dark color of her nipple.

"Your breasts are beautiful," he murmured, before he reverently pulled one turgid tip into his mouth. He sipped delicately; then, when her skin's honeyed sweetness flooded across his taste buds, he suckled long and hard.

"Don't stop," she moaned, when she felt his mouth leave her breast.

"I could," he whispered, ever vigilant to reassure her that he could stop at her slightest inclination. "But I won't. Not until you've had enough."

Alana vaguely realized she wanted these pleasurable sensations to continue forever. Only in the far recesses of her mind did she hear an unrelenting beeping noise. Her head shook wildly from side to side in an effort to silence it.

She heard Sylas groan; she felt her blouse being drawn together. She pried her eyelids apart in time to see him reach for the intercom button on the telephone.

"Kincaid, here." His voice was harsh, abrupt.

Damn! he silently cursed. If this is Gregory, so help me God I'll dissolve the partnership!

"Leslie Faye is in the waiting room. She says she needs to see Alana," Carmela calmly announced.

"We're extremely busy." Sylas made a valiant effort to make his voice sound businesslike, but in his present state of passion, he wasn't mentally perspicacious enough to think of a valid reason to bar Leslie Faye from his office. "Can she wait until later to talk to Alana?"

"It won't take long," Leslie Faye piped, loudly enough for Alana and Sylas to hear.

Alana caved into the seat of her desk chair. Her equilibrium was muddled by the rampant desire still percolating throughout her body. She fumbled with the clasp of her bra. Her brown eyes widened in silent appeal for Sylas to get her a few minutes in which to repair her clothing before Leslie Faye barged into the office.

"Give us a couple of minutes to finish tallying these statistics. I'll buzz through to you."

Alana ran her fingers over her blouse front to make certain it was buttoned correctly. Remembering how she'd unmercifully teased Leslie Faye when she'd returned to the dorm from a date with Gregory with her sweater on backward, she chuckled softly.

"What's so funny?" Sylas considered himself to have a good sense of humor, but Leslie Faye's untimely interruption was no laughing matter. He muttered under his breath, "I thought patience was a virtue to be rewarded!"

"You've got lipstick on your mouth," Alana answered, keeping her private thoughts.

"You don't."

Alana pulled her purse from the bottom drawer of the desk and removed a mirror, a comb and a tube of lipstick. She hastily applied coral color to her lips. Although her hairstyle was simple, she couldn't completely restore it in a couple of minutes.

Sylas scrubbed his mouth with a tissue. "Did I get it?"

"Yes. Do I look presentable?"

His eyes narrowed when he noticed the rumpled state of her blouse. "You look as though you've been thoroughly kissed. You might want to put your suit jacket on."

One glance at the deep creases in her blouse and Alana blushed to the roots of her dark hair. She pulled her jacket off the back of her chair, slipping her arms inside the sleeves.

"Ready?"

"Ready," Alana replied.

Sylas pushed the button. "Send her in, Carmela.'

The directive barely passed his lips when Leslie Faye threw open the door and rushed to Alana. She had two jewelry boxes in her hand.

"Take your pick. I have a customer at the store waiting for me. Whichever pair you don't want to wear to the cocktail party, she wants to buy."

"You should have let your regular customer have first choice." Behind Leslie Faye she saw Sylas point to Leslie Faye's neck and make a wringing gesture. Alana fought to keep from laughing. She opened both boxes. One held large, navy-blue button earrings, surrounded in bands of rhinestones. "These are a bit larger than I usually wear."

"They're gorgeous!"

"Compared to these, the button ones are tiny." Alana held up a pàir of four-inch dangling blue stones next to her ear. "Which do you like the most, Sylas?"

"Either pair will look fabulous on you," he said extravagantly.

"See!" Leslie Faye crowed, clapping her hands. "Sylas has impeccable taste. I told you they were gorgeous."

Alana put the dangly earring back in the box and handed it to Leslie Faye. "I think the buttons are the more conservative pair. Was there another reason for your dropping by?"

"Nope. You've been too busy to come by the store and make a selection." She wheeled around and gave Sylas a saucy grin. Alana noticed suddenly that there was a trace of lipstick on his collar. She blushed. Leslie Faye gave him a big hug and continued, "So, since tonight is the big night for you two, I thought I'd better make an emergency office visit."

"That was very thoughtful of you, Leslie Faye," Alana said. "Thanks. Now, if you'll excuse us, we have to go over these figures or we'll be working late and miss the party."

Leslie Faye giggled as she lifted the point of Sylas's collar. "By all means, continue with whatever you were doing." She stepped back and gave both of them a look Cupid would have been proud of. "I must say, this looks very promising. Very, *very* promising."

"Scat!" Alana ordered, grinning at her friend's outrageous impudence. She moved around her desk to escort Leslie Faye to the inner office door. "I'll see you back at your place."

Leslie Faye put her arm around Alana's waist and gave it a squeeze. In a whisper, she said, "I've waited ten years to get even with you for that comment you made about me having my sweater on inside out."

"Backward," Alana corrected.

"Inside out. I clearly remember it being inside out."

"Okay," Alana agreed, willing to compromise. "Inside out and backward."

She shooed Leslie Faye out the door, shut it then turned around toward Sylas.

"What was all that whispering about?"

"Girl talk."

Sylas closed the space between them in four long strides. "*Is* tonight the big night?"

She knew what he meant. Her tongue flicked over the roof of her mouth as shivers of excitement formed goose bumps on her arms. Those long, luscious kisses of his had awakened her sexuality.

But was she ready to take the next step?

She'd unburdened her soul to him. Sylas Kincaid shared her secret. She'd expected any man who heard what had happened to her to think the same thing the majority of the people they'd surveyed had thought— a woman raped on a date got what she deserved.

But Sylas wasn't just any man.

He'd listened. He'd set her thinking straight. She'd been naive, but not stupid. She was the victim, not the perpetrator. She had nothing to be ashamed of. She shouldn't feel guilty.

Tonight would be more than her first date in a decade. She wanted to willingly share with Sylas the part of her that she'd anesthetized with hard work.

Simply put, she realized, she'd fallen in love with him. Sexuality was a part of her love. She wanted to be closer to him than she'd been with any man. She wanted to share with Sylas what had been taken from her forcibly by Tom Lane.

"Yeah. I think maybe tonight is the big night."

Chapter Ten

"Are you sure you don't want to double with us?" Leslie Faye asked as the doorbell chimed. "Gregory has promised to be on his best behavior with you."

"Get the door and stop fussing, would you?"

Alana was as nervous as a bird about to take flight from the top of a skyscraper. Leslie Faye's acting like a mother hen for the past two hours hadn't helped.

"He can wait a second or two," Leslie Faye replied. "It's good for him. Heaven knows I spent years twiddling my thumbs waiting for him."

She gave Alana a final motherly once-over. From the sophisticated strapless chiffon jumpsuit and sparkling earrings, to the flowery perfume she'd laced Alana's bathwater with, her friend appeared and smelled absolutely breath-taking.

Satisfied with her handiwork, Leslie Faye opened the door.

Alana was turning to leave the room to avoid watching Gregory and Leslie Faye kiss, when she heard Gregory call her name.

"Yes?" She watched Leslie Faye nudge him toward her. What was her friend up to? Gregory had kept his distance from her since their last spat, and that suited her just fine.

"Why don't you two have a little chat while I fix Gregory a martini?" Leslie Faye offered, beating a hasty retreat to the kitchen.

"Leslie Faye wants the two of us to be friends," he stated without preamble. "I do, too."

Uncharitably, Alana wondered how many hours he'd had to practice in front of a mirror before he'd been able to push those words through his lips.

Gregory shoved his hands in the pockets of his dark trousers. He mumbled, "I've always been jealous of the relationship between you two."

Stunned by his confession, Alana blurted incredulously, "Why?"

"Because I thought the friendship you two shared was more important to Leslie Faye than what she felt for me."

Alana watched for subversive body movements, but his eyes were directly on her. He appeared abashed by what he'd said, and yet he also appeared earnest. She decided to say nothing until he finished.

"I know I can be self-centered. And I know that once you were out of the picture, I smugly felt that Leslie Faye was completely mine." He glanced toward the kitchen, then back to Alana. "And I also know that my shamefully neglecting her is what caused her to date men like Ed Morgan after she divorced me.

I've made mistakes. Bad ones. But I'm trying to change.''

Alana nodded to let him know she'd heard him and to encourage him to go on.

"Leslie Faye isn't my possession. I can't stick her up on a shelf and expect her to be waiting for me when I get home. By secluding her, I thought she wouldn't have any choice but to love me. I guess I treated her that way to hide my own insecurities.''

Leslie Faye's return to the living room with his drink only momentarily stopped him. He kissed his wife's forehead and spoke to her as well as Alana.

"I've always been afraid Leslie Faye would love someone more than she loved me.''

"And that's why he's been ugly to you, Alana.'' Leslie Faye wrapped one arm around Gregory and gestured for Alana to come closer, until her other arm was around Alana's waist. "I love both of you—my husband and my best friend.''

Gregory closed the circle by draping his arm across Alana's shoulders. "Do you think you can forgive me for the nasty things I've said about you?''

"You'll have to forgive me for being openly hostile toward you.'' She hugged his waist. As she stepped away from the two of them, she added, "Does this mean you're considering a reconciliation?''

Leslie Faye's blue eyes twinkled. "The bride wore stripes? The newly married couple booked a honeymoon suite at the state penitentiary? They conceived their first child through a plate-glass window?''

"You, my dear X-rated wife, have an irreverent sense of humor.'' Gregory erased the sting of chastisement by dropping a kiss on her mouth. "Did I tell you your mouth has a distinctly sassy flavor?''

Grinning, Leslie Faye replied, "Better sassy than submissive?"

"Yep. Sweet and tart and feisty."

Their congenial bickering continued until they reached the front door.

"See you at the party...friend," Gregory said, smiling genuinely at Alana.

After she heard them go down the wooden steps, Alana took a long look at herself in the mirror. Leslie Faye had changed far more than her outward appearance. She smiled at her reflection.

She felt beautiful, inside and out, thanks to Leslie Faye.

Her friend's influence had directly and indirectly changed her life. Friendship had brought her back to Texas. By working on Leslie Faye's case, Alana had been forced to lower the defenses she'd built.

Her conscience was cleared of guilt feelings. She could face herself in the mirror and not be ashamed of what she saw. She'd never be a nineteen-year-old virgin again, but she could be a whole woman.

Best of all, Leslie Faye had introduced her to Sylas Kincaid.

She hugged herself and twirled around in exuberance. She hadn't felt this good in years!

Unable to stay pent up inside the condo while she waited, she picked up the beaded purse Leslie Faye had lent her and opened the door.

Sylas had his finger an inch from the bell when the door swung back. One look at Alana and his heart lodged in his throat. Graceful and beautiful were the twin adjectives that burned in his mind.

"Hi. Must have been ESP," she joked, giving him a special smile reserved just for him. "Great minds on the same wavelength?"

"You look absolutely beautiful."

"Jinx!" She snapped her fingers the same way she and Leslie Faye had done when they were kids and said the same thing simultaneously. "I was thinking you look beautiful, too."

Sylas made a wry face as he reached for the knot in his tie. "First I'm cute and now I'm beautiful. Shall I loosen my tie and muss my hair?"

"Only if I get to brand you with lipstick on your collar before we go to the cocktail party," she replied saucily. "I don't want to have to shoot dirty looks at all the women who see how sexy you are."

"Since men don't wear lipstick, I guess I'll have to give you a passion mark to keep the men away from you." He touched her pulse point. "Right about here."

A tingle radiated from where he lightly touched her. She felt aglow from head to toe as she basked in the warmth of his gaze.

Sylas spread his fingers across her bare shoulders and drew her close to him. "I wouldn't bruise you with my kisses. You're precious to me."

"Am I?" Her lips parted, inviting him to kiss her.

Sylas was only too happy to oblige.

Since she'd left the office he'd done little but think about kissing her. And his thoughts hadn't stopped there.

He'd thought about making love to her.

Her single sexual experience had been a disaster. He wanted to prove to Alana that lovemaking could be magnificent.

Mentally he'd rehearsed how he'd give her pleasure. Slowly. patiently. He'd kiss every inch of her. He'd touch her in ways guaranteed to please her.

And then, when he'd physically reacted to the mental images of their lovemaking, he'd taken a cold shower and wondered if his patience could tolerate the strain without shattering into tiny pieces.

"We'd better go," he said, feeling his face flushed with his inner heat. She had no idea how her slightest touch was like throwing gasoline on the flames roaring inside of him.

She wanted to linger. "There's no rush, is there?"

"I'm trying to avoid rushing you," he admitted with blunt candor. His eyes glanced from the front room toward the hallway leading to her bedroom. He reached behind her and closed the door to the apartment firmly, before his libido overpowered his control. "Unless you don't want to go at all, I think we'd better leave."

Disappointment mingled with heightened anticipation in Alana as she removed his handkerchief from his pocket and dabbed at the trace of lipstick on the fullness of his lower lip. She folded the hankie and returned it to his breast pocket.

"I guess we should make a token appearance. Otherwise, Leslie Faye and Gregory will be pounding on the door wanting to know if I chickened out at the last minute."

Sylas took her hand and tucked it into the crook of his elbow. "Gregory mentioned something about skipping dinner because he'd be eating humble pie tonight. Any idea what he meant?"

"Peace talks with the enemy." She pointed to herself. "I suspect that I'll be getting a second invitation to be a bridesmaid in the near future."

He groaned out loud. "Does that mean I'll have to be best man? Again?"

"Probably. Maybe that old cliché about always a bridesmaid and never a bride goes for best men, too," she teased, not feeling the least bit sympathetic.

Sylas considered giving her a playful pat on the rear end and making a smart comeback, but he decided he'd be smarter to keep his hands to himself.

"I hope they do remarry."

"You aren't afraid she'll be making the same mistake twice?"

"Gregory has made some mistakes, but he loves her. She loves him. The biggest mistake they could possibly make is to *not* remarry."

Alana wanted Leslie Faye to get her fondest wish. After she was found not guilty at the trial, everything would be back to normal in her life.

As they neared the steps, Sylas straightened his arm and gestured for Alana to precede him. The soft swishing of chiffon against satin, the feminine sway of her hips, the hint of floral perfume clinging to her skin made him reckless.

"Alana."

His voice echoed in the stairwell. At the landing, she stopped and turned around. Why hadn't he followed her?

"Yes?"

"Are you nervous about tonight?"

Uncertain whether he was referring to the party or the intense awareness between them, she replied, "I'll probably know the majority of the people there."

"What about after the party?"

Alana placed her hand on the rail and started down the next flight of stairs. "I'm taking it one step at a time."

"Then I'm way ahead of you."

She glanced over her shoulder and smiled up at him. "I knew you would be. I'm counting on it."

She sounded cool, confident, certain that what she felt for Sylas was stronger than irrational fears. If love had the power to heal, to make wrongs right, then tomorrow she'd awaken in his arms and the past would no longer dominate her life.

"Alana Benton! Is that you, darlin'?" Ruby Cameron rushed to greet Alana by folding her into her arms. She drew back and took a long hard look at Alana through her wire-framed bifocals. "Good Lord, child, it's been so long since you've been around this neck of the woods I thought you were dead and buried."

"It's good to see you, Mrs. Cameron," Alana said, pleased to be remembered by her parents' elderly friend. Ruby had to be pushing eighty, from the other side, Alana mused. Being the driving force on several charity committees must have kept her younger than her years. "Have you met Sylas Kincaid?"

"Why, sure. How are you, Sylas? Won any million-dollar settlements lately?" She held up her cheek for Sylas to kiss. Not waiting for Sylas to reply, she turned toward Alana. "How are your folks? Still hiding out in the hill country? Why is it people live in one place all their lives, and up and move when they retire? Does that make any sense to you?"

Alana grinned. Ruby could fire questions faster than a gunslinger could shoot. "My folks are fine. They miss Galveston as much as I have."

"Would you excuse me for a minute, Alana?" Sylas asked in a low voice. "A client over by the bar is motioning for me to join him."

Before Alana could answer, she was being pulled away from Sylas. "Don't you fret about Alana," Mrs. Cameron said, taking Alana by the wrist. "There's a whole bunch of people at my table who are going to be tickled pink to see her."

Smiling, Alana wiggled her fingers at Sylas. She'd sat on her father's knee at enough political get-togethers to know there was often more business conducted at a social function than in an office.

"I saw Leslie Faye and her husband, that is, ex-husband, earlier." Mrs. Cameron's nose tilted upward. "I don't understand these modern-day divorces. If my Albert started talking divorce around me, I'd start talking about his final resting place at the cemetery!"

Alana followed Mrs. Cameron as she wound her way among several tables, nodding and smiling at her acquaintances. A sociologist would love being here, Alana thought, noticing how the rich and powerful pillars of Galveston society were seated at a large table in the center of the room. As if they had ladders propped against the pillars, clusters of social climbers circled the table.

"Look who's came home!" Mrs. Cameron grandly announced. "Albert, you remember Alana Benton, don't you?"

Albert Cameron rose from his chair. He stepped between the women, draped his arms across their shoulders and gave each of them a Texas-size squeeze. "Of course, dear. How could I forget one of my bank's prettiest customers? My, my, child, you're all grown-up! Sophisticated! How long has it been since you begged the tellers at the bank for orange lollipops? More years than I'd want to count?"

Nodding, Alana said, "More years than *I'd* want to count. You're looking as handsome as ever, Mr. Cameron." Remembering how her father used to say that a man couldn't get a loan without having to listen to one of Albert Cameron's jokes, she added, "Heard any good jokes lately?"

Tossing back his head, Mr. Cameron laughed. "You remember, huh? You always were a sweetie pie. Ruby, didn't we read something about Alana in one of the national newsmagazines?"

Alana felt her face growing warm when she noticed the people who'd been chatting with nearby friends had stopped talking and had turned toward her. She glanced around the room, searching for Sylas. She needed to be rescued before someone asked her whose case she was working on and what it was about. Leslie Faye would be mortified if she heard everyone gossiping about her.

"Why, yes! Now that you mention it, I do remember you commenting on how glad you were to see a local girl make a name for herself." She looked at Alana, but lowered her voice to make certain everyone listened. "You work with attorneys, helping them pick good jurors, don't you? Is that why you're with Sylas Kincaid? Why don't you let me introduce you to the bank's attorney and a few big-shot attorneys who are here from Houston?"

"Whoa, Ruby!" Albert tickled Alana's ribs the way he had when she was a child. "Did you hear the one about the blind jackrabbit and the blind snake?"

Alana shook her head. Surreptitiously, she continued to look for Sylas.

"Well, these two creatures bumped into each other out in the desert near the Panhandle," Mr. Cameron began. "For a few minutes neither of them said anything 'cause they were so scared. But finally the jackrabbit said, 'I'm blind. Would you be kind enough to tell me what you are?' The snake kind of slithered around and said, 'I'm blind, too. I don't know what I am.' Well, they both thought and they thought, until the rabbit said, 'Maybe we could touch each other until we figured out what we are.' The snake cozied up real close. 'Well,' he said, 'you're fuzzy, with long ears and a fluffy tail. I'd say you're a jackrabbit.' The rabbit thumped its back leg with joy, then touched the snake. 'You've got beady eyes, a forked tongue and no spine.'" Albert began to guffaw. "'You must be a lawyer!'"

Alana had heard a bawdy version of the same joke from a female attorney, but she laughed along with the others at the table, some of whom she would have bet were attorneys. Her laughter changed to a choking sound as her eyes locked on a group of men and women who'd been standing behind Mr. Cameron. Color flooded her cheeks.

Mrs. Cameron patted Alana's back. "Oh dear, she was laughing so hard, she must have swallowed down the wrong pipe." She picked up the glass closest to her, and said, "Drink this."

Whiskey fumes warned Alana of the potency of the drink, but she downed it in one gulp. She needed it.

Tom Lane stood less than twenty feet away from her.

Before she could gather her wits, Mr. Cameron had pulled out his chair and insisted she take it.

"I'm fine," she whispered. The Scotch she'd belted down had robbed her vocal cords of their ability to make a sound and had hit her stomach like a sledge-hammer. She needed a minute to recover her poise, without making a scene. "Please, really, I'm fine."

A man across the table said, "That story of yours reminds me of the bank robbers who were planning to pull the biggest heist of the century, right here at Albert's bank."

Ruby grinned. "Judge Tyler, shame on you. You wouldn't tell a banker joke to get even with Albert, would you?" Without causing further commotion, she moved a glass of ice water in front of Alana.

Tom Lane! Alana shuddered, tuning out the voices around her. He wasn't in Lower Slobovia! Damn his soul, he was in Galveston! What if he saw her? What if he recognized her?

Her eyes circled the large room frantically. She couldn't find Sylas. Sylas! she screamed silently. Get me out of here! She had the overwhelming urge to push back her chair and run. She'd be supplying grist for the gossip mill, but she didn't care.

She could feel her heart beginning to pound. Her lips were tightly compressed. She was breathing in short, erratic gasps through her nose. She clamped her teeth on the soft inner lining of her bottom lip to quiet her silent screaming before it erupted between her lips.

Like Mr. Cameron's rabbit, she felt mesmerized by a snake. She knew she shouldn't look at Tom, but her eyes were drawn back to him. He still looked the same.

Tall. Blond. Muscular build. Repressing a shiver, she wondered if Tom had a picture in the attic of his house, like Dorian Gray, that grew increasingly grotesque with each victim he attacked. Dammit, he should at least have become bald and paunchy!

She wondered if she should do exactly what judge Tyler was doing to Albert Cameron—get even.

Her eyes squeezed shut as she remembered the destructive fantasies she'd spun like a lethal spider's web around Tom Lane. The first few weeks she'd been alone and scared in Missouri, she'd fabricated what had happened in Tom's dorm room. When he pushed her on the bed, she'd opened her mouth and screamed! Men from the adjoining rooms had broken through the door. Tom had been hauled off her and thrown out in the hall. It had been Tom who suffered at the hands of his friends. It had been Tom who was tarred and feathered and run out of town.

A couple of years later, her fantasy had changed when she received Leslie Faye's letter inviting her to be her bridesmaid. She had pictured herself dressed in a ghostly white gown circulating from one woman to another, telling them what happened to women who went out with Tom Lane. She had her revenge when he asked every one of those woman for a date and they all refused him.

There had been other fantasies. A common thread had run through each of them—revenge!

Here, right now, at this instant, she realized, she had her opportunity to expose Tom Lane. She could destroy him socially and professionally. He'd never be able to show his face in Galveston again!

A burst of laughter shattered Alana's private thoughts. She forced herself to smile as though she'd enjoyed Judge Tyler's joke.

"Over your coughing spell?" Mrs. Cameron asked. "You look frightfully pale. Can I get you something?"

"No. Thanks." She managed to garner up another weak smile. "If you'll excuse me, I do think I'll start searching for Sylas. He may be outside getting a breath of fresh air."

"Sylas Kincaid is a fine young man, Alana. A real catch for some smart lady," Mr. Cameron said, assisting her from her chair. "Since he's a friend of yours, I think I'll mention his name at the bank's board of directors' meeting this month."

"I'm sure he'd appreciate the bank's business, Mr. Cameron."

Alana turned toward the French doors that led outside. She hadn't the slightest intention of passing through them. Shoulders back, head held high, she moved toward the circle where Tom Lane stood.

"Alana! Over here!" Leslie Faye beckoned Alana to join her.

Making certain she kept an eye on Tom, Alana veered across the room toward Leslie Faye.

"Do you mind staying at the condo by yourself tonight?" Leslie Faye asked in a lowered but bubbly voice. "I think tonight is going to be *my* big night. Gregory has been on the verge of popping the question all evening! He invited me to his place after the party."

Alana did mind. She wanted to confide in Leslie Faye, to explain why she'd taken action tonight, before her friend heard what happened secondhand. She desperately needed to talk to her, but Alana couldn't selfishly put her peace of mind above Leslie Faye's happiness.

"No, I don't mind."

"Are you looking for Sylas? I just saw him over in that direction with a glamorous redhead putting the make on him. You'd better go stake your claim."

"In a minute." She couldn't allow herself to think about how Sylas would react to what she was about to do. "I recognized someone on the opposite side of the room I need to speak to."

"Oh? Who?"

Leslie Faye rose on tiptoe; Alana moved sideways and blocked her view. Her friend might remember that Alana had once had a crush on Tom. Knowing her tendency to play matchmaker between Sylas and Alana, she didn't want Leslie Faye jumping to the wrong conclusion. She would haul Sylas over there pronto, if she thought Alana was expressing interest in another man.

"A professional acquaintance from Houston," Alana lied. "Don't worry. He's ugly as sin." To her, he was exactly that.

"Come back and join our group when you've finished talking business. I want everybody to meet you," Leslie Faye urged.

Alana nodded, unwilling to compound her lie with an empty promise. After she thoroughly humiliated Tom Lane, none of Leslie Faye's friends would be interested in socializing with her.

She was dead set on making a spectacle of him. He so richly deserved it!

Chapter Eleven

Sylas half listened to the redhead spilling out her marital woes. He'd watched Alana reluctantly be the center of attention at the Camerons' table. Poised, beautiful, gracious, Alana charmed Albert Cameron until Sylas feared his gray eyes would turn green with jealousy. He wanted to be at her side.

When she was seized by a series of coughs, he'd wanted to rush to her aid, but at that particular moment the woman beside him had her fire-engine-red fingernails buried in his coat sleeve. As Alana zigzagged around the tables, after leaving the Camerons' party, she paused to speak to Leslie Faye, then continued moving through the crowded room. He raised his hand to get her attention.

Disheartened that she had missed his gesture, he observed her approaching a small group of men and women on the outer fringes of the room. After the warm reception she'd received so far from Galveston's elite, he wondered why her shoulders were squared back. He noticed she was holding herself rigid, with no feminine sway of her hips.

Something was wrong. He could feel it.

"...and Jonathan must be running around on me. Two nights of the week he phones and makes excuses about working late." The redhead fluffed her curly hair and struck a seductive pose. "Do you think I should be worried?"

Sylas hated being flagrantly discourteous, so he turned his attention back to the woman who'd been making broad hints about being bored with her husband. "Isn't that Jonathan over by the dance floor, trying to get your attention? I believe the band is about to start. Would you excuse me?"

Before she could sink her claws into him again, he sidestepped around her and moved toward Alana, who was now at the edge of the tightly knit group.

Alana was waiting impatiently for the right moment to exact her revenge.

"What about the home for abused women, Tom?" a woman who stood to his left asked. "Have you managed to get enough private funding to continue operations?"

"Yes. Barely. We may have to cut back the length of time a woman can stay there, though." His hand raked through his hair and his brow furrowed into deep creases. "We should be extending the services instead of cutting back."

"The publicity coming out in the Sunday *Houston Post* should help the cause."

Alana stared at the woman who'd softly spoken. Her hand was resting in a familiar manner low on

Tom's back. Her thick glasses and straight, plainly cut brown hair gave her an owlish appearance. Alana glimpsed a small diamond and a wide gold band on her ring finger. Tom's wife? This studious-looking woman wasn't the type she'd pictured with Tom Lane.

As she listened to the serious exchange on the topic of battered women, she took another hard look at Tom. Did Tom have a twin? She couldn't imagine the man who'd sexually abused her being concerned about abused wives. What had caused such a radical change?

"Legislation is what's needed," Tom said, his face grim. "Funding the house to shelter these women won't stop the men's abusive behavior. Do you all realize that more than half the men arrested had at one time or another witnessed their mothers being beaten? We need a comprehensive program to reeducate these men and their children. This is a vicious cycle that's perpetuated from one generation to the next."

Caught up in what he'd said, realizing she had made a similar statement to a legislator in Wyoming, Alana felt her desire to wreak havoc on Tom Lane slowly ebbing.

He'd hurt her, but how many women had he helped?

She pushed the unwelcome thought aside. This man had been the monster in her hellish nightmares! He was directly responsible for the mental agony she'd suffered. She parted her lips to speak. Before she could begin the hateful speech she'd silently rehearsed over the past decade, her conscience stabbed her. Her mouth clamped shut.

She'd hated him, he'd earned her hatred, but the thought of destroying the man's reputation in public left a sour taste in her mouth.

"I think we ought to lock these guys up and throw away the key," the woman standing beside Alana muttered. "That'd break the cycle. Everybody knows those men won't change. Once a wife beater, always a wife beater."

Tom turned toward the woman who'd spoken. Alana felt his eyes pass over her to the speaker, then bounce back to her. She watched his face turn brick red. Half a second later, his skin blanched to a deathly paleness.

"Men can change," Tom said, his voice sincere, never breaking eye contact with Alana. "I've felt deeply ashamed for a wrong I once committed. At that time, I wanted to make amends, but sometimes face-to-face apologies are prevented. The person may refuse to take a phone call, or read a letter, or they may leave town without a trace. Guilt feelings and remorse can be powerful motivators prodding a man to make changes in his thinking, in his actions."

Sylas touched Alana's elbow to let her know he was beside her. He expected her to flash him one of her heart-stopping smiles, but she continued to stare at Tom Lane, the man Sylas considered the county's biggest do-gooder.

Sylas had been watching her as he crossed the room and had noticed how her stubborn chin was set, ready for a fight. She'd looked at Tom Lane as though he were a cockroach she wanted to squash. But her expression had changed when Tom said men could change. She'd looked bewildered, but slowly that look had faded, as if each word Tom spoke was one more step toward solving some complicated puzzle.

Sylas narrowed his eyes. Only he heard Alana whisper, "Apology accepted."

His gut twisted. Ancient primitive instincts ignited inside him, threatening to burst through the thin veneer of civilized behavior. Was this the man who had violated Alana? A red haze of anger blurred Sylas's vision. He rapidly blinked his eyes to clear it.

Tom moved toward Alana; he extended his right hand. Sylas stepped between the two of them and took Tom's hand. He had to control the muscles in his own to keep from pulverizing Tom Lane's knuckles. If his suspicions were correct, a horsewhipping on the courthouse steps was the mildest punishment Sylas wanted to administer to Tom.

He felt Alana lightly touch his coat sleeve.

"Sylas, would you mind taking me home?" Beneath her hand, his forearm felt as hard as a rock. His gray eyes had the glitter of finely honed steel. She knew he must have guessed the identity of the man in the story she'd confided to him. She couldn't forgive Tom yet; she'd held on to her rage too long for it to be erased with a simple apology. But she didn't want Sylas to defend her by provoking a fight. In a whisper that she hoped no one else could hear, she said, "Please. This isn't your problem. It's mine."

"It's our problem," Sylas replied, wanting to take full responsibility for seeking justice on her behalf. He'd been attracted to Alana for her intelligence, strength and beauty, but he now realized how much he loved her for her compassion.

He dropped Tom's hand as though slime oozed between the man's fingers. He abhorred hypocrites. But more than that, he'd felt an instant enmity toward the man who'd stolen Alana's innocence and condemned her to live in an emotionless shell, exiled from her home and the people she loved.

Alana and Sylas drifted toward the door to the area where he'd parked the car. They'd barely stepped into the courtyard when Alana turned and encircled his waist with her arms.

To avoid being interrupted by people coming and going, Sylas moved off the sidewalk. Palms and oleanders obscured them from view. Moonbeams filtered through the palm leaves, casting silver light on them.

"I wanted to punch him," Sylas growled. He held her snugly against his chest. "Damned hypocrite! He's fooled all of us. Do you realize half of this city wants to nominate him for the state legislature and the other half thinks he should be put up for sainthood?"

Alana sighed, melting against Sylas, feeling completely safe and secure. "Shh, Sylas."

"Don't shush me. I'm furious. You should have exposed him for the louse he is."

"Was," Alana corrected. "Once."

Sylas wasn't mollified. He wanted to give Tom something the man would remember ten years down the road. Then he might be able to feel compassionate toward him, but right now he wanted blood.

Inhaling deeply, Alana began to sort through her emotions. "Remember my telling you how outraged I was when Tom tried to contact me? It never crossed my mind that he felt guilt or remorse. If he had crawled on his knees for ten miles and humbly apologized, I wouldn't have believed him." She raised her head until she could see Sylas's eyes. "But how can I argue with solid proof? He's founded a shelter for battered women."

"And a couple of halfway houses, too," Sylas admitted begrudgingly. "But his good deeds don't change what he did to you."

"No, but they change my viewpoint of who I am. Don't you realize the reason I never dated was because I thought I was a poor judge of character when it came to men? I couldn't trust my own judgment. I hated him and I hated myself. But Tom Lane isn't a monster and I'm not a dim-witted floozy!"

"Nobody would think that of you."

"I thought it. As long as I have this inner rage concerning Tom Lane, I'm stoking the same inner rage I feel about myself. So that leaves me with two options. I can keep hating him and keep hating myself…or I can forgive Tom, and forgive myself, too."

Sylas placed his hands along both sides of her face. "But can you forget what happened?"

"I can do my level best to try and forget what happened. I'd like to begin tonight." She stood on tiptoe and brushed her mouth against his. Her hand reached up to smooth his wrinkled brow. "I know what you're thinking. Yeah, I'm a little scared. Maybe that's to be expected." She took his hand and placed it on her heart. "But I have faith in my own judgment. In here, I know you're a fine, decent man, Sylas Kincaid. I trust you with all my heart."

Sylas threaded his hand through her hair until he reached the clasp that held it at her nape. A flick of the thumb and he released the clasp. He tucked it into his jacket pocket, then lifted the ends of her hair until the silky strands blew free in the wind coming off the Gulf.

"I'm falling in love with you, Alana. Does that scare you?"

"No. I feel the same about you."

"Say it," he coaxed, his lips coming closer and closer to hers. "Tell me you love me."

"I love you, Sylas." Instinctively, she knew he wanted something more from her. "I want to make love with you."

His hands settled low on her back as his lips covered hers. He cradled their hips together, languorously swaying as gently as the palm tree fronds overhead. His tongue danced across her lips in time to the music coming from inside the hotel. In the silent language of lovers, his body told her what he couldn't put in words. He wanted her, needed her. She was as precious to him as the air he breathed.

Alana responded as though that wintry night ten years ago had never occurred. Her hands ached to stroke Sylas as he had touched her in his office. Her mind was curious to know if his body would respond involuntarily, as hers had.

Alana ended the kiss. She smiled up at him. "Take me home?"

"My home." His face lit up; the thought of Alana in his home pleased him. He took her hand as they strolled unhurriedly toward his car. "I like the idea of waking up with your head on the pillow next to mine."

"With your arms around me?"

Her steps lightly kept pace with his. She felt as though she floated on air. She'd felt this way once before, with Tom, but she wasn't afraid. She savored each and every bubble of joy bursting inside her veins.

"Throughout the night," he promised, grinning at the prospect. "Tomorrow's Saturday, so we can sleep in late. That is, of course, if you don't want to go into the office to work."

"I wasn't a workaholic by choice, only out of necessity," she replied pertly.

Sylas faked a groan. "Does that mean that after tonight I'll have to drag you to work?"

"Maybe," she teased. "Or maybe I'll be the one with my foot in the middle of your back, shoving you out of bed."

Chuckling, Sylas took her conjecture a step further. "Or better yet, maybe the charges will be dropped and we won't have to worry about going to the office."

"Or..." She paused while her imagination took flight. Her dark eyes full of laughter, she lifted his hand over her head and twirled in a circle beneath it. "Maybe what I'm feeling this very instant is contagious. It'll spread around the world before we wake up in the morning. The bad guys will join the ranks of the good guys, and the jury consultants, lawyers and judges will retire."

Impossibilities seem possible tonight, Sylas thought, a bemused smile curving his lips.

He reached in his pocket for the keys to his car.

Within ten minutes, he unlocked the front door of his home and ushered Alana inside. She closed the door while he flicked on the light switches. One glance at the furnishings told Alana he took as much pride in his house as he did in his work.

She ran her fingers up the front of his shirt until she reached his tie. One long tug later, she draped it on the doorknob. She stepped out of one shoe, then the other, while Sylas removed his jacket. She took it from his hand and draped it across the back of a tapestry-covered chair.

By the time they reached his bedroom upstairs, a trail of clothing haphazardly decorated the furniture, floor and banister.

Amused by Alana's abandoned behavior, so untypical of her, he asked, "Leaving a trail in case we get lost?"

"Uh-uh."

She didn't know how to explain her actions without sounding odd. She wanted to break the rigid control that had governed her every waking moment—from how she organized the food on her plate to how she neatly folded her clothes before putting them in the dirty clothes basket.

She crossed to Sylas's king-size bed. Subconsciously she noted it was twice the size of the bed in the dorm room. Out of habit, she started to test the mattress for firmness. Silently she groaned. Twenty-nine years old, standing in the middle of a man's bedroom dressed only in her lingerie, and she was more concerned about good back support than she was about the man in the room with her?

She felt so damned inadequate.

"Nervous?" Wearing only his trousers, Sylas leaned against the doorjamb. He thought her overt gestures belied her inner turmoil. She hadn't so much as glanced at him since they'd left the top landing of the stairs. She needs time and space, he told himself. It was profoundly important to him that nothing he did even faintly resembled what she'd described as her only experience.

Yes! she longed to tell him. "No," she said.

"I am."

Alana's head snapped up. She twisted at the waist toward him. "You're nervous? Why?"

"Mmm. I'm watching you break the tiny rules in your life like matchsticks. I'm wondering why. Tell me what you're feeling."

Her hand fluttered to her bare throat. She backed away from the bed toward him. Courageously, she made an effort to laugh at her ineptness. "I'm feeling like a high school dropout who's taking the bar exam!"

Sylas remembered how he'd felt at his bar exam, as though his entire future depended on his score. Pass or fail. No middle ground.

Or was there?

A law student could pass parts of the exam and retake the parts he failed.

Sylas made a snap decision he hoped would allay the fears of them both.

Confidently taking the initiative, he crossed the room to side of the bed and pulled back the top sheet and coverlet. With his back to her, he shed his trousers, then slid between the sheets.

Alana recoiled inwardly. She worried her bottom lip between her teeth. She listened for the small warning voice inside her, telling her to get out while she still could. She heard only the steady beating of her heart.

Feminine intuition told her she'd pushed his patience and her courage to the limit. She had to make a decision and stick to it.

Sylas patted the bed beside him, then opened his arms and revealed the decision he'd made to her. "Let me hold you, Alana. It's what we both really need."

"I thought you brought me here to make love to me."

Silently she wondered if this was some sort of trick? A variation of what Tom had done. Would Sylas lure her into his bed with promises of hugs, then pin her under him and ... No! her mind yelled. Trust him!

She took a tentative step toward the foot of the bed.

"I did," he replied honestly. He dropped his outstretched arms to the coverlet. "But I thought you wanted to come here to make love *with* me. I won't lie to you and say I'm perfectly content with the idea of our only sleeping together. But then on the other hand, I'm completely opposed to the idea of my bed being the testing ground for your womanhood."

Alana moved forward another couple of steps. Was it in the realm of possibility for a man and woman who were physically attracted to each other to share a bed without making love?

"Won't you get ... frustrated?"

His eyes locked with hers. "You know I'm a patient man."

"But isn't this different?" She put one knee on the mattress. "Once I'm beside you, won't you want to finish what we started back in your office?"

"I could lie to you and say no." His gray eyes delved deeply into her brown eyes until he felt as though what he was about to say would be indelibly imprinted on her soul. "Make no mistake about this, Alana. I want you. I want to kiss you all over, then bury myself so deeply inside of you that our hearts become one. Judging from how you respond to me, I think that's what you want eventually, too."

When he witnessed a rosy tinge spreading across her cheeks, he wondered if he'd been too explicit. He'd gone too far to stop without leaving room for misunderstandings.

"But what's the rush? Isn't holding each other, building a solid foundation of honesty and trust between us, more important than sexual gratification? Sex is only one way of expressing love.''

She sank down onto the bed, stretching out on her side next to him.

Several inches separated her body from his.

"Trust me, Alana. I won't hurt you.''

She believed him.

He saw her faith in him glowing in her eyes. He slid his arms beneath the curve of her waist and slowly closed the gap between them.

Chapter Twelve

Sylas looped the sheet over her. His lips grazed her forehead; he peppered tender kisses along her nose and chin.

For a moment, just a moment, her mind flashed back to another bed, another man.

He felt a tremor race through her. "It's only natural to remember," he whispered.

"Why did the bubble of happiness I felt while we were driving over here burst the minute I walked into your bedroom?"

He lightly tapped her temple with his forefinger. "Up here, you've consciously absolved your guilt feelings, but subconsciously you're reacting to being in a similar situation. It's like people who survive a natural disaster, like a hurricane or a tornado. When the wind picks up, rationally they know they aren't in danger, but their defense mechanism goes on alert."

"I don't hear any warning voices." She nuzzled against the mat of hair on his chest. It tickled her nose; she rubbed it, then splayed her fingers through the crisp hair. Unaware of doing so, her toe trekked up his leg to his knee, then back to his ankle. "Do you think I'll always freeze up?"

She freezes, Sylas mused wryly, and I'm getting hotter and hotter. He shifted to his back, letting her half sprawl across him. His hands lazily shimmied across her back. He fervently hoped his patience would last until his inner fires could thaw her.

"No. You won't always freeze. You've taken the most difficult step. You're here beside me in my bed, voluntarily."

Long into the night Sylas held Alana. He talked about growing up on a ranch, chuckling as he counted the shenanigans he and his brother had pulled. In return, she related stories about Leslie Faye and herself. Lengthy silences punctuated the tales they told. During the quiet times, he absorbed the floral fragrance and texture of her skin. She explored the vast differences and subtle similarities between their bodies and marveled at how her soft curves fit perfectly against his hard, lean body.

The grandfather clock downstairs chimed twice when Alana had to stifle her first yawn. Curled up against Sylas, at peace with herself, she drifted asleep.

Sylas stared at the ceiling, listening to the sounds of the night. A whippoorwill's call mingled with the purr of an occasional car passing on the street.

He doubted that Alana realized the impact of her innocent explorations on his libido. He ached. The sheet on the far side of the bed had to be permanently wrinkled from being clenched in his hand. He couldn't count the number of times he'd clamped his lips together or chuckled to conceal a low groan.

There has to be something to that cliché about suffering making a person stronger, Sylas mused. He felt as though he'd single-handedly wrestled with Alana's demons and won.

For now it was enough to be sharing the same bed, listening to the muffled sound of her breathing. A small grin of contentment lifted one corner of his lips.

He wondered if this was how a married couple spent the night on their fiftieth wedding anniversary—wrapped closely together, nestled in the haven of each other's arms. This wasn't what he'd thought would be bliss, but it was damned close!

As his last thought before sleep claimed him, he mumbled against the crown of Alana's hair, "I love you."

A weight lying heavily across the small of her back prevented Alana from rolling to the side of the bed. Momentarily disoriented, which was not uncommon since she seldom slept in the same place for more than a couple of weeks, she drowsily tried to get up to answer nature's call.

Slowly she opened one eye. She stared into a forest of dark hair. Her head lifted, her eyes popped open and then she smiled, remembering that she'd slept with Sylas! His chest had been her pillow. His arm had held her against him throughout the night, as he'd promised.

Wide awake, she slowly eased away from him until she was off his bed. She stood beside it and let her eyes drink their fill of him.

Asleep he looked like the young rascal he'd depicted in his anecdotes, except for his overnight growth of whiskers. His tousled dark hair made her fingers itch to touch it. Sooty lashes cast shadows beneath his eyes.

Her eyes scanned the wide V of hair on his chest to where it disappeared beneath the sheet. While she watched, he rolled to his side. Her cheeks flamed as she caught herself hoping the top sheet wouldn't completely cover him.

As quietly as possible, she moved to the bedroom door. What she saw when she stepped into the hallway caused her eyes to widen and her cheeks to flush. A high-heeled shoe dropped in the entrance hall, her jacket flung on the back of a chair, her jumpsuit draped carelessly on the banister. Sylas must have parachuted his white shirt from the steps; it lay spread-eagled in the middle of the living room carpet.

She smothered a girlish giggle. As soon as she took care of business in the bathroom, she'd clean up the mess they'd made.

Sylas cuddled Alana's pillow in his arms. He inhaled deeply and rubbed his whiskers against the sleek satin. She felt so soft. Too soft, the thought slowly registered in his dream-laden mind.

Eyes opening, he pushed the pillow away from his chest. "Alana?"

He swept aside the sheet and sat up. Where was she? He cocked his head to one side listening for her.

"Alana!"

He picked up his slacks and hastily shoved his legs into them. She'd gone! Where? He dug one hand into his pocket. His keys were still there. Why hadn't she wakened him? Surely she hadn't walked to Leslie Faye's condo.

"Must have taken a taxi," he muttered, silently tacking on a mild expletive.

There was only one explanation he could think of for her vanishing into thin air—shame.

He picked up the telephone on the nightstand. His finger shook as he punched in Leslie Faye's number. The phone purred in his ear twice.

"Alana?"

"We're sorry," a recorded voice recited, "but we cannot connect your call as dialed. Please—"

Sylas slammed down the receiver, then directed his entire concentration on pushing the correct buttons.

"Who are you calling at this hour in the morning?" Alana asked. She rolled up the sleeves of his plaid robe, which she'd found hanging on a hook in the bathroom.

"You!" Sylas growled. He sprang off the bed. "Where'd you go?"

Alana chuckled. "To the bathroom." She bared her teeth. "I hope you didn't mind me filching a new toothbrush from your drawer."

"I thought you'd gone."

Uncertain of what he considered proper bedroom protocol, she asked, "Did you want me to leave?"

"Hell, no!" He pulled her into his arms for a bear hug. "I woke up, clutching your pillow like a teddy bear, found you were gone and started jumping to conclusions."

She leaned back in the cradle of his arms and hopscotched her finger down the side of his face. His whiskers reminded her of bristles on a brush.

"Are you always this grouchy in the morning?"

"No." Sylas laughed. She had no way of knowing how amorous a man felt in the morning. His hand skimmed from her shoulders to her hips. Unless he was about to set a record for making his second mistake of the day, before coffee, she wore less beneath his robe than she'd worn to bed.

"What's so funny?"

"You are."

"Why?"

He slid the tip of his finger down her nose. "Ask me tomorrow morning. What time is it?"

"A little after six."

"So much for sleeping late," he groused.

Her brows lifted slightly. "Maybe you ought to go back to bed and get up on the other side. You're as grouchy as a grizzly bear with a thorn in his paw."

Far from being insulted, he thought she'd come up with a terrific idea. He scooped her into his arms, stalked to the side of the bed and dropped her in the center of it.

"That wasn't a hint," Alana said, laughing as he shucked his trousers. He crawled in beside her and pulled the sheet up over both their heads. "You're what my grandmama used to call 'a little tetched in the head.'"

"Yeah, but you love me anyway, huh?" Not waiting for her response, he said, "I should have shaved. I probably *look* like a grizzly bear, too."

"Uh-uh." In the semidarkness, she moved closer as though she couldn't see him. "More like a porcupine."

"A cute porcupine, I suppose?" His fingers strummed across her ribs. "Woman, you're trampling on my male ego!"

She grabbed for his hand, laughing as he continued to tickle her mercilessly. "Okay. I'm sorry. You don't look like a cute porcupine."

He stopped. The way she was squirming against him would have a disastrous effect on their platonic relationship if he continued to tickle her.

Alana braced her arms against his shoulders to make a speedy escape after delivering a punchline. "Whoever heard of a cute porcupine? They're homely as sin!"

She was quick, but Sylas was quicker. He circled her waist and pulled her fully on top of him. Playfully he scoured her upper chest with his chin. "I'm gonna give you an ugly-as-sin porcupine burn."

What had started as fun came to an abrupt end when the knot tied at her waist came loose.

"Beauty and the beast," Sylas whispered, his mouth suddenly as dry as the desert wind. "We'd better stop."

She deterred him from closing the front of the robe by lowering herself against him. She gasped. The rasp of his hair on the tips of her breasts felt heavenly.

A low groan that seemed to come from the tip of his toes rumbled through his chest, and then passed through his lips.

For an instant, she thought she'd hurt him. She glanced upward. His throat worked; beads of perspiration gave a slick sheen to his upper lip. His eyes were bright.

He curved his hands around her bottom and rocked her against him. "You thought I laughed at you when you asked if I was always a grouch in the morning. The joke is on me, sweetheart. Men are vulnerable in the early hours of the morning. I'm sorry, Alana, but I don't trust my self-control.''

"I trust you," she whispered, forgetting everything except how she yearned to have him kiss her, hard, passionately. She braced her hands against the mattress and moved directly over him. "Make love *with* me, Sylas. Make everything right for me."

He didn't have to be asked twice. His hand darted to her nape. He took possession of her mouth; his tongue drove between her lips and teeth until he felt the velvet texture of her tongue. A zesty peppermint flavor exploded across his tongue.

The passion he unleashed in her took Alana by surprise. Her fingers dug into his shoulders. Her tongue tangoed with his, darting, swirling, thrusting with long sure strokes.

Did he push back the sheet? Did she shed his robe?

Stunned by the force of her desire, she didn't know or care. All she was aware of were the hard muscles beneath his supple skin, the gentleness of his hands as they washed over her. She clung to him, moaning softly, wanting something, anything to relieve the ache building at the juncture of her thighs.

Sylas broke their kiss. He clasped her shoulders in his hands and lifted her away from him. His gray eyes burned into hers with a silent question. He'd never forced a woman; he wasn't about to take her unless she wanted him.

"Yes," she chanted, "yes, yes, yes."

"Straddle my waist with your knees," he whispered urgently. "Let me see you, touch you. See me. Touch me."

While her fingers clenched his biceps, his hands flowed down her arms to her hips, then upward to the womanly swell of her breasts. He kneaded them the way he had in his office, because he knew it aroused her.

He rose to his elbows; she lowered her shoulders to accommodate him. He laved one nipple with his hot, moist tongue, then devoted equal attention to the other. His hands moved to her waist; he lowered his shoulders back to the pillow, bringing her directly above him.

Alana moved like a kitten being stroked. Her shoulders rotated; her hips swayed. His gift of love was her freedom of movement. She set the pace and was in control.

Tom had denied her that privilege by pinning her to the bed with his weight. Against her will, he'd taken her.

The unwelcome thought knotted her stomach with anxiety. Sylas could use his strength against her, too. He could lose control. He could force himself into her until she felt as though she'd been ripped apart.

Her arms stiffened; her hips ceased to sway. Her eyes opened wide to make certain her nightmare hadn't come to life.

Sylas felt her pliancy change to rigidity. He pulled her against him and whispered, "I love you, Alana. Don't think of past hurts, just feel my love. Do you want me to stop?"

"No!"

Tears of frustration welled in her eyes. She longed to cry out . . . Sylas, make me a whole woman!

And yet, from deep within her came an insight that silenced her plea. Sylas couldn't make her a whole woman. She, and only she, had the power to become whole. She could stop him and cower in her hopeless fears forever, or she could face those fears, go beyond them and become all that she could be. Sylas could help her, but in the end, she was the only one who could make herself whole.

She flattened herself against him, sliding to one side of him. She began to explore him with a thoroughness born from a desire to abolish her fear of the unknown. Womanly instincts and his responses told her where and how to touch him. He echoed her strokes until her dark eyes burned with passion.

Her fingers folded around him, and he gave a harsh groan as his patience neared its limit. His hips arched rhythmically as he kissed her wildly, hotly, hungrily, and his breathing became ragged as his tongue matched the pace of her hand and his hips.

"Move over me," he said, his voice hoarse with passion. His hands guided her until her knees were astride his hips. The heel of his hand nestled in the feminine curls between her thighs while he reached to the drawer of the nightstand and prepared to protect her from pregnancy. He languidly rotated his hand, parting her, seeking her heat, her moistness, until he felt certain she was ready for him.

"Feel me against you?"

He held himself close to her until she could no longer bear the waiting and pressed against him.

"Yes, sweetheart. Take me inside of you. It's where you want me." Sylas feared his patience would snap when she arched her hips, straightened above him and slowly sank down on him. His natural urge was to drive his hips upward until he completely sheathed himself inside of her. He held his hips perfectly still.

Alana gave a sharp gasp of pleasure as she relaxed and felt herself stretch to accommodate him. She'd expected pain; there was only pleasure. Slowly, at first, she rocked against him, then as the pressure inside of her began to build, she moved faster. She marveled at the fantastic sensations spiraling upward, into her.

Although she was the dominant force in their love-making, his body language quickly cued her movements. She thrust against him, hard, when she felt his hips arch; she slowed when his hands languidly stroked her hips, breasts and shoulders. Her entire body became attuned to her needs and his.

Sylas meant to be infinitely patient and gentle. He'd have sworn on a stack of Bibles that he could have been, but he wasn't prepared for Alana's unbridled desire.

"Now, love," Sylas called urgently. His arms folded her against him. He rained hot, moist kisses on the wetness he felt on her cheeks. He felt her shudder as the final vestiges of passion swept over both of them.

It seemed hours later that Alana felt his lips gently nibbling at her neck. She smiled. "I had no idea making love would be like that," she whispered, awestruck.

Sylas chuckled. "Can you tell me how you feel?"

"This isn't the time to ask open-ended questions, counselor," she chided lightly, unable to put her feelings into coherent sentences.

"Believe me, cross-examination is the last thing on my mind." He tucked her shoulder under his arm and rolled to his side so he could see her face. If he lived to be one hundred, he knew he'd cherish the memory of the wonderment he saw in her eyes. "Shall I tell you how you make me feel?"

"Can you? I seem to be tongue-tied."

He dropped tiny kisses along her brow. "You make me feel very, very special."

"You are special." She painted the dark whiskers above his upper lip with the tip of her fingers. "Simply the best. I wish...I wish I'd met you sooner. Do you think if I'd been Leslie Faye's bridesmaid we'd have been together sooner?"

Sylas hesitated, not wanting to dampen the feeling of bliss they shared. He didn't think she would have been ready to deal with love then. And until he'd researched Leslie Faye's case, he wouldn't have known how to deal with her problem, either.

"Fate, thy name is Leslie Faye," he teased, choosing to laugh rather than cry over what they might have missed. "Are we star-crossed lovers?"

Alana smiled smugly. Her long legs tangled with his as she cradled her hips against him. Only a woman who'd been deprived of physical love could understand the sweet flavor that coated her tongue as she whispered, "Lovers."

Chapter Thirteen

Let's say you're at the point where you've explained the procedure of the trial, you've told them you aren't looking for fairness and impartiality—only honest answers and complete openness—and you've asked several jurors questions.'' Alana checked off the items they'd previously covered with a red pen. She looked up at Sylas. "You notice one of the jurors shakes like a schoolkid who hasn't done his homework every time you ask a question of anyone sitting near him. What would you say to him?"

Pensively, Sylas rubbed his chin with his forefinger. The closer they came to the trial date the more Alana pinpointed specific behavior. "I'd reassure him that it's okay to be a little nervous. I'd admit that I'm nervous, too, because I'm responsible for what happens to my client in her immediate future."

"That makes him aware that you relate to him as one human being to another. We hope you will have accomplished that earlier. Does it allow him to reveal anything about himself?"

"No." Sylas shook his head in frustration. "I should say something like, 'Mr. Didn't-Do-Your-Homework, you appear nervous. Tell me what's making you feel that way.'"

Alana grinned. "Substitute the man's real name and your question is perfect. It demands a response. Okay, let's say one of the information sheets states that Ms. Hudson is married to an FBI agent. Give me a series of leading questions that will reveal her attitude about her husband and about law enforcement, and any predisposition toward the defendant."

The intercom buzzer sounded. "Saved by the bell," Sylas said as he picked up the telephone. "Yes, Carmela?"

Alana pointed to the door, silently asking if she should leave. Leslie Faye wasn't his only client. There had been occasions when she'd vacated his office to give him the privacy he needed to discuss business with other clients.

"Put him on the line," Sylas instructed. He raised his hand, shaking his head to stop Alana. "Yes, Mr. Collier. What can I do for you?"

The prosecuting attorney? Alana wondered if the status of Leslie Faye's case had changed.

"I see." Sylas listened carefully. He jotted on a legal pad: PLEA BARGAIN? GUILTY AS CHARGED. SUSPENDED SENTENCE. PROBATION. He held up the note for Alana to read.

"No!" Alana mouthed. "Drop the charges."

"Mr. Morgan is feeling benevolent?" Sylas repeated Collier's remarks for Alana's benefit.

Alana made a thumbs-down signal.

"In Mr. Morgan's present frame of mine, perhaps he'd be willing to drop the charges." Sylas frowned. "Yes. I agree. The county's tax dollars should be spent judiciously. I'll contact Mrs. Hale and get back with you. Thank you for calling."

"What a jerk!" Alana couldn't believe the P.A. would contact Sylas with such an absurd offer. No way in hell would she allow Leslie Faye to plead guilty!

"He's just doing his job."

Too antsy to remain seated, she jumped to her feet and marched to the side of Sylas's desk. "Leslie Faye will never agree to this. Not if I have any say in the matter—which I will."

"I gather you're going to recommend that we reject Ed Morgan's benevolence?"

"You gathered right, counselor. I won't allow Leslie Faye to be victimized twice, once by Ed Morgan and the second time by having to assume guilt in public."

Sylas studied the block letters he'd made on the legal pad. He tapped his fingers on the words *suspended sentence*, then pushed back his chair and looked up at Alana. "In actuality, a suspended sentence is little more than a legal slap on the wrist. Leslie Faye did injure the man."

"But she was defending herself!"

"Agreed. But if she accepts this offer, her primary concern—going to jail—will be alleviated. It'll be over for her."

"No." It wouldn't be over. Alana slammed her fist against her palm. "Dammit, no! The offer is unacceptable."

Sylas pushed himself to his feet. He went to her and put his hands on her shoulders. "Alana, sweetheart, think about this. It isn't like you to make a snap decision when you haven't examined the final consequences."

"The consequences haven't changed." She held up her hand and raised a finger with each statement. "We go to trial. Leslie Faye is found *not guilty* of all charges, and then she can decide whether or not she wants to press charges against Ed Morgan." Her thumb and forefinger circled into the okay signal when she finished.

"If we can take all that for granted, then why have we been working twelve hours a day preparing for this case?"

"It's our preparation that will lead to the final decision."

"Alana, you've read the survey results. You know the chances are only fifty-fifty for an acquittal."

Her dark eyes burned brightly with passion. "That's without the two of us influencing what takes place in the courtroom. We up the odds in our favor."

"*Our* favor? Alana, this is our case, but you aren't the one going on trial."

Alana's heart slammed against her ribs as his remark hit its target. "You're damned right it isn't me on trial. But it could have been me. Maybe it should have been me."

"But it isn't. You're taking this personally. It isn't your freedom that's in jeopardy. It's Leslie Faye who will have to serve time in prison if I can't convince the jurors their beliefs about date rape are wrong."

Frustrated, expecting compassion from him on her behalf, Alana swiped his hands from her shoulders. "You're a man! You'll never be able to understand how I feel about this case!"

"I'm the man who loves you, Alana," Sylas said softly. "I thought you'd made peace with Tom and with yourself. Make me understand how you feel."

She turned away from him. She wanted to scream at him. Her throat worked hard to swallow the hot tears sliding down the back of it. "I don't want Leslie Faye's name besmirched with filthy lies."

"Leslie Faye's name? If this case doesn't go to trial, no one other than her ex-husband, you and me will ever know about the attempted rape. If anything, we'll be protecting her name."

Alana pressed her knuckles against her bottom lip. She couldn't argue with his logic. She'd run far and fast to keep anyone and everyone from discovering what had happened to her. How could she, in good conscience, ask Leslie Faye to get on the witness stand and give a blow-by-blow account of Ed Morgan's attempt to rape her?

But Leslie Faye isn't a scared nineteen-year-old, she silently argued. She's a grown woman who knows what she wants. Hadn't Leslie Faye said she wanted her life to return to normal? Being convicted of assault and battery, having a criminal record, wasn't normal. Leslie Faye wanted her name cleared! Gregory's name, too!

"There's far more at stake than not being incarcerated. She wants to remarry Gregory." Alana crossed to the window that overlooked the Gulf and pulled back the sheer drape as though by doing so she could shed light on the situation. "You know about Gregory's political ambitions. He wants to be governor of Texas eventually. Think, Sylas! Think about the long-range consequences of plea bargaining. She'll have a criminal record. Political opponents thrive on scandals. Do you think Gregory will remarry her at the risk of his future political career?" Alana made an indelicate snort. "Not the Gregory I know."

Sylas raked his hand through his hair, wondering if Alana had thrown Gregory into the disagreement as a red herring. He knew her ego was intertwined with the facts in this case. And he also knew she was hurting, but he couldn't let the feelings she refused to share with him affect his judgment as a lawyer.

"If what you say is true—and mind you, I'm not certain it is—then Gregory doesn't love her. He let his career come between them once. He's made adjustments in his life-style. Isn't there a slim possibility that he won't make the same mistake twice?"

"No," she replied stubbornly.

Silently Sylas groaned. "Is that a fair judgment?"

Alana dropped the curtain and turned away from the window. Her eyes locked with his. He met her fierce glare without blinking an eye.

"You want to talk about fair? Is it fair to ask Leslie Faye to plead guilty to assault and battery charges when she was defending her honor? That's fair?"

"Let's not debate the fairness of the legal system, okay? I'll admit it's not fair, but it is a solution to Leslie Faye's problem."

"No, it's a temporary relief—like my running away. The pain will haunt Leslie Faye the same way it haunted me. It changed my life. It'll change hers, too. She'll always wonder if she was cowardly."

Certain he was getting closer to how Alana felt, he asked, "Is that what bothers you, Alana?"

She raised her chin as though she could take any blow he cared to deliver, but her insides churned. "What bothers me is your questioning my professional and personal judgment. Aside from the fact that I'm confident we can win, I'm also Leslie Faye's best friend. No one knows her better than I do. Do you think I'm stupid? I've been through this. Don't you think I know what's best for her?"

"I believe you may be too close to the situation to view it clearly," he replied truthfully. "Have you told Leslie Faye you were raped?"

"Of course not," Alana snapped.

"Why? Isn't she your best friend?"

"It's because she is my friend that I haven't burdened her with my problems. Don't you think she has enough to worry about?"

"I think you're underrating her strength."

And mine, he silently added. From the rigidity of her spine to the thrust of her chin she reeked of defiance. Not only did she have myopic vision regarding their case, she'd also blurred the line between their personal and professional relationship. That made him want to pull her into his arms and kiss her until she realized that his advice to Leslie Faye had nothing to do with how he felt about her.

Alana folded her arms across her waist to keep a grip on her composure. Was she letting her experience taint her judgment? Was she balking because she sincerely felt Leslie Faye would be making a grave mistake to accept the prosecuting attorney's offer? Oh

God, she thought, hugging herself tightly, am I asking my friend to do what I couldn't do?

Sylas picked up the telephone receiver. "Do you want me to call Leslie Faye, or do you want to call her?"

Fearing that there were elements of truth in his accusations, Alana shrugged. She detested the thought of being unable to trust her own judgment. "You're her legal counsel—counsel her."

Alana felt tears gathering in her eyes. She looked upward to prevent them from sliding down her cheeks. She wouldn't cry. Not here. Not in Sylas's office. Her feet weighed a ton as she moved to her desk to get her car keys.

"You're her friend. She'll want your input."

"I'll give her my two cents' worth when she comes home."

"Do you object to my having Gregory in on the consultation?"

She forced a weak smile. "You do what you think is best."

Sylas banged down the receiver, crossed the room in three long strides and pulled her against him. "This may not be the best thing to do, but by damn I'm not going to let you crawl back into your shell without putting up one hell of a fight!"

She turned her face away from him. If he kissed her, she knew she'd weaken. "No."

Sylas flinched, but refused to release her. "No, don't kiss me? No, don't call Leslie Faye? Or no, don't love me? You have them all mixed together."

Alana felt certain she'd choke on her own tears. She longed to take back her refusal. She needed to be held, kissed, loved, but she'd be foolish to admit it.

"You're hurting me."

Sylas saw shadows of pain in her eyes. A sick feeling settled in his stomach. His hands dropped to his sides.

"You're hurting yourself," he whispered, "and there isn't a damn thing I can do about it."

She stumbled through the door, terrified that Sylas Kincaid knew her better than she knew herself. She had to get away from the office to sift the facts, separate them from her emotions.

"Alana, could I speak to you for a moment?" Gregory asked as she passed his office.

"Later." She blinked. A teardrop splashed on her cheek. "Much later."

Gregory rounded his desk, but he was too late to stop her. He glanced toward his partner's office. Sylas stood in the doorway looking as though he'd lost his last friend.

"What the hell is going on around here?" Gregory demanded.

"A professional disagreement over Avery Collier's willingness to accept a plea bargain in Leslie Faye's case."

"Oh, yeah?" Gregory strode across the hall into Sylas's office. "What are the terms?"

Sylas watched Alana disappear through the front door, then turned toward Gregory. "Leslie Faye pleads guilty as charged. Collier recommends a suspended sentence."

"That's his first offer?"

"First and final offer. Morgan thinks he's being benevolent and Collier says he's saving the taxpayer's dollar." Sylas circled his desk and returned to his chair. "Alana is opposed to accepting the offer. What do you think?"

"I think I smell a rat," Gregory said slowly. "The bad boys down at the pool hall have been razzing Ed Morgan for allowing a pint-size female to beat him up. They're saying Morgan wants revenge for the scar Leslie Faye put on his face. Considering those facts, I can't imagine Morgan dropping the case out of kind-heartedness."

"Collier being worried about the taxpayer's dollar is a complete about-face for him, too."

Talk about not seeing the forest for the trees, Sylas silently chastised himself. He should have been questioning the motivation behind the prosecuting attorney's unexpected call rather than being side-tracked by Alana's emotional upheaval.

Sylas picked up his pencil and doodled Collier's name on his legal pad. "A month ago Collier thought this was an open-and-shut case. He wouldn't be backing off now unless something unforeseen had happened."

"My exact thoughts," Gregory agreed.

"What about the private detective Alana suggested you hire. Have you heard anything from him?"

"He interviewed some of Morgan's neighbors. Nothing we didn't already know about there. But who knows? His snooping around may be the motive behind Collier's plea-bargain offer."

Sylas chewed thoughtfully on the pencil's eraser. "I'm going to call Collier and stall him. In the meantime, Leslie Faye should be informed of the offer. Alana strongly opposes accepting any deals. What's your recommendation?"

"No deal." Gregory shoved his hands in his pockets. "I haven't changed my mind. I still think you can win the case." A small smile stole across his face. "Do you realize Alana Benton and I are finally agreeing on something?"

"Yeah, that's got to set some sort of record. But I'm seriously concerned about the risk of taking this case to trial," Sylas warned. "Leslie Faye's primary fear is going to jail. She can accept Collier's offer and be rid of that worry."

"You talk to her. Tell her I'm checking on some loose ends. See what she says." Gregory headed toward his office. "Give her my opinion, too."

Sylas picked up the phone. Under his breath he muttered, "Thanks a lot, ol' buddy." Gregory and Alana champion her cause, he thought, while I feel like a heel for considering taking Collier's offer. And yet I'm the one making the phone call. Thanks for nothing!

Alana removed her heels and tossed them in the back seat of her car. During the short drive to the condo, she'd called herself everything from a selfish bitch to a weak, spineless jellyfish. Angry with herself, she kicked puffs of sand with her toes as she crossed the dunes to the beach.

She wondered what had happened to the cool, composed, rational woman who stepped off the plane at Hobby Airport? Until she returned to Texas, she'd compartmentalized everything into neat, tidy pigeonholes. She'd prided herself on being thorough, logical, reasonable.

"Dammit, I was in control!" she grumbled. "My life was disciplined, regimented. What's happened to me?"

Back in Sylas's office, she'd been irrational and unreasonable. She'd exploded at him before she'd methodically considered the pros and cons of accepting Collier's offer.

"Why?"

She couldn't bear to think about how she'd rebuffed Sylas. That made a circle of pain band around her heart until she felt tears burn her eyes. She'd deal with her personal problems after she analyzed what had caused her passionate rejection of Collier's offer.

Alana grimaced as her big toe struck the edge of a broken oyster shell, but she continued to follow the tide line.

She hated to admit it, but she was beginning to wonder if her abrupt rejection stemmed from a secret desire, one she hadn't consciously acknowledged, to make Ed Morgan the sacrificial lamb for all men who abused women? From the beginning, she'd made no bones about telling Leslie Faye that once acquitted, she should press charges against Morgan.

As Alana stared down at the flotsam washed ashore by the waves, a picture formed in her mind of a faceless man behind bars, wearing prison garb.

"Yeah," she conceded. She did want all rapists put behind bars. "But at what price?"

She'd told Sylas she thought Leslie Faye should take the risk of being found guilty, but in all truthfulness, she hadn't let that prospect weigh on her mind. Conceit or self-confidence? she wondered. She had faith in her ability. Her track record with apparently no-win cases was impressive, but that didn't guarantee an acquittal.

She lifted her face to the sun. The yellow light and the blue sky reminded her of Leslie Faye's curly blond hair and blue eyes. Alana detested the idea of her friend's pleading guilty, of her being branded with a criminal record, of her having to report to a parole officer.

But she couldn't trust her own bias when Leslie Faye's freedom was at stake.

Only Leslie Faye could make the choice.

"Bias," Alana mused aloud. "It's a good thing I'm not on jury duty. My name would be red-lined by the defense attorney instantly!"

Her predisposition against Ed Morgan had partially caused the change in her usual systematic behavior. Without having laid eyes on the man, she'd hated him with the same passion she'd hated Tom Lane. While her attitude toward Tom had changed because of their encounter at the party, it hadn't fluctuated one iota toward Ed Morgan. It would still give her enormous pleasure to see Morgan behind bars. Then she'd know he wasn't out forcing his attentions on other unsuspecting women.

She whirled around to face the condominiums when she heard her name blowing in the wind. Leslie Faye stood on the balcony waving at her. She waved back, gesturing for Leslie Faye to join her on the beach. She saw her nod, then run lightly down the wooden steps.

As Leslie Faye ran toward her, she knew how Peter Pan felt when he said he never wanted to grow up. If she and Leslie Faye were still youngsters, their biggest concerns would be sand castles and pirates' treasure.

"A far cry from prisons or personal defeats," Alana mumbled.

"Hey, Princess Alana! What are you doing down here?"

Alana had to grin at Leslie Faye's choice of names. "I'm contemplating my sins."

"Plan on being here for a while, huh?" Leslie Faye teased, a little out of breath from the run. She fell into step beside Alana. "Sylas called."

"He told you about Collier's offer?"

"Yeah. Both you and Gregory think accepting the offer is a crummy idea, so—" she lifted her shoulders as though the weight of the decision had been removed from them "—I told Sylas to call Collier and tell him to take his plea and shove it. Sylas said he wants to stall him for a day or two until Gregory checks out some loose ends."

Leslie Faye beamed a smile at Alana to remove the troubled look from her friend's face. "I can't have you flying down here like an avenging angel and then say, 'Oops, home safe. You'd never return another one of my calls if I cried wolf, would you?"

"No, I'm always available if you need me," Alana contradicted, feeling very unangelic.

Since Alana had decided not to influence Leslie Faye's decision, she felt relieved that Collier hadn't been given a final rejection. As they walked side by side, she decided Leslie Faye had a right to know any advice she might give would be tinged by her personal bias.

"Leslie Faye, there's something I think you ought to know."

"That you and Sylas had a fight? So what?" She linked her arm through Alana's. "Think of the fun you'll have making up!"

"Be serious, will you?"

"Lighten up," Leslie Faye countered, laughing at Alana's long face. "It's too gorgeous a day to be morose. Anyone watching the two of us would think you're the one being fitted for a prison suit."

"Will you stop cracking prison jokes? You aren't making what I have to say easy."

"Okay." She mirrored Alana's grim expression, but her eyes lit with laughter. "I'm duly somber. Fire when ready."

While Leslie Faye joked around, Alana had searched for a delicate way to tell what had happened to her, but she'd failed. Bluntly, she said, "I'm a victim of date rape."

Leslie Faye's heels dug into the sand as she rocked backward. "Oh my God, Alana! I'm so sorry." Her hands fluttered helplessly for a moment, and then she wrapped her arms around Alana, hugging her. "This case must have been a dreadful ordeal for you. I always worried about you traveling from one big city to another by yourself. Who knows what kind of crazy weirdos you meet up with?"

"It happened while we were roommates." She watched Leslie Faye's expressive face turn absolutely white. "It's why I left Texas and moved to Missouri."

Leslie Faye dropped her arms from around Alana. "Why didn't you tell me?"

"I didn't tell anyone. Not you. Not my parents. No one."

"Why?"

Alana shrugged her shoulders. "I couldn't talk about it."

"Dammit, that isn't good enough. Why did you shut me out of your life!"

Sighing heavily, Alana answered in a small voice, "Because I felt stupid and ashamed."

"Stupid? Ashamed?" Leslie Faye repeated, as though she couldn't assimilate the words. She backed away from Alana. "Is that why you never came back? Not even for my wedding? The most important day of my life?"

"I didn't stay away to hurt you." Alana reached out to Leslie Faye. "I was hurting so badly I didn't think about how you'd feel."

Leslie Faye pressed her fingers to her temples. She blinked rapidly. "You had no right to keep silent. Dammit, we shared everything with each other! You've always felt you had to be the strong one—superior to me. That's why you didn't want to tell me! Your stiff-necked pride kept you silent!"

"That's not true," Alana denied, horrified. "I wasn't thinking straight. I just wanted to run and run and run!"

"For ten years?"

"Yes! After a while, I couldn't pick up the phone and say, 'Oh, by the way, a couple of weeks before I moved, I went out with a guy for hamburgers and he raped me!'"

"Why haven't you told me before today?"

"I didn't want to upset you."

"Upset me!" Leslie Faye roared. "I'm going on trial. *Me! Me!* Don't you think I feel stupid? Ashamed? Knowing you've been through this might have helped me! You let me down, Alana!"

"I didn't. I came when you called me. You're the only reason I came back."

Leslie Faye pushed her hand against Alana's shoulder. "You had no right to withdraw from our friendship without telling me why! For months after you left I felt guilty, wondering if I'd done or said something terrible! I felt like I'd had an arm or a leg amputated!" She pushed Alana again. Tears spurted from her eyes. Her voice cracked as she shouted, "D-d-do you know how I spent the weeks before my birthday and Christmas? Pestering the m-mailman! Waiting for your card, hoping you weren't too busy to write a letter? D-d-damn you, didn't you know I cared, that I'd have done just about anything to keep our friendship alive?"

"It didn't die! I caught myself talking to you as though you were with me. I thought I'd go crazy!" Alana's arm made a wide arc. "I cried enough tears to fill the ocean, but I just couldn't come back and I couldn't tell you why."

Leslie Faye wheeled around and made a dash toward the condo. "I hate you, Alana. I want you out of here...out of Texas. I hope I never hear your name or see you again!"

"You don't mean that!"

Alana chased after her. Although Alana's legs were longer, Leslie Faye's anger gave her the impetus to run faster. Alana's heart pounded so hard she thought it would burst. Or break, she didn't know which. She stopped at the edge of the dunes and watched Leslie Faye dart up the steps.

"Leslie Faye! Please try to understand," she pleaded. Her fingers intertwined; she clenched the heels of her hands together. "I thought I was punishing myself for being stupid! I didn't mean to hurt you!"

Leslie Faye stopped at the first landing and shouted, "Go to hell!"

Chapter Fourteen

Alana groaned. She sank to her knees in the sand. She'd survived ten years in her own private hell; she sincerely doubted she had the strength to go on alone. She truly felt stupid not to have realized she'd hurt her friend. Ashamed of her insensitivity, she didn't have the vaguest idea how to right the wrong she'd done her.

"Here's the album I've kept about your successes," Leslie Faye shouted. She threw a thick, green leather volume from the balcony. The wind caught the binder, opening it and tearing pages from it. "Being your friend made me feel important. When Gregory worked late night after night, I'd go through the pages and pretend I was you! I needed you then, too! And when I was getting my divorce I thought I was dying inside. I needed you to say, 'Yeah, that'll get his attention,' or 'Don't be impetuous,' or simply, 'I'm here, Leslie Faye. I'll stick by you right or wrong because I'm your friend!' But all I heard from you was the empty sound of silence.''

She untied a blue ribbon from around a stack of envelopes. ''I would read your letters and cards! I saved them all, but I don't want them anymore.'' She pitched them a few at a time until they pelted around Alana like paper squares of rain. ''I believed in you, Alana. I admired you. I trusted you. But you betrayed me. All those years while we were growing up I thought I was the luckiest kid alive to have you for my best friend. I should've known you were too good to be a true friend!''

Alana watched speechlessly while her friend tossed the mementos over the railing. She lowered her dark eyes to the first batch Leslie Faye had thrown. Her fingers trembled as she picked up an envelope yellowed with age. She read the date on the postmark and knew it was the first letter she'd written Leslie Faye after she moved. Her heart twisted in anguish as she remembered how many pages of stationery she'd wadded up and thrown away before she'd been able to complete one page without staining it with tears.

She looked up, wanting Leslie Faye to see the misery on her face.

''And here's one more thing.'' Leslie Faye dropped a carton of small-size Cokes over the railing. ''I always did prefer Pepsi!''

Her friend's final gesture gave Alana a glimmer of hope. Her tears slid to the corners of her mouth as she smiled sadly. In the worst battle the two of them had had, Leslie Faye had thrown Alana's doll's evening dresses down the clothes chute and declared they'd never play dolls again. Later that same day, Leslie Faye had crawled through Alana's bedroom window with the dresses in her hand, and though she'd acted as if nothing had happened, she'd had her doll apologize to Alana's.

Leslie Faye had always had a terrible temper when she was riled, but she'd be sweet as carnival cotton candy within twenty-four hours.

"I can wait," Alana whispered, tucking the letter in the front of her dress.

Unsteadily, she jackknifed to her feet. The Gulf breeze blew Leslie Faye's memorabilia helter-skelter along the beach. For a moment, Alana considered salvaging as much of it as she could, but she had second thoughts.

There was so much heartache attached to the mementos, both her own heartache and Leslie Faye's, maybe it was better to let them blow away. While her friend was collecting them, she'd put Alana on a pedestal. Now that Leslie Faye knew they suffered from the same human frailties, it would be better if they could start fresh.

Tomorrow, she'd be at Leslie Faye's door with a peace offering.

She'd been wrong to exclude Leslie Faye when she was troubled. Then something Alana hadn't thought of before made her shiver. If she'd confided in Leslie Faye when they were roommates, her friend might have avoided the situation with Ed Morgan. Leslie Faye's painful ordeal could have been prevented.

Alana extracted her keys from her purse, wishing she could rewrite the past. Knowing what she knew now, she'd have revised more than her experience with Tom Lane.

She climbed into the car and started the engine before she realized she had no place to go.

"Yes, you do," she whispered, backing the car from the parking space and turning from the parking lot toward town. "Leslie Faye isn't the only person who deserves an explanation."

She'd unfairly attempted to eliminate Sylas from her life, too. As she sped toward town she fervently prayed his compassion was stronger than the anger he'd justifiably directed at her.

She'd attached contingency strings to the love she'd offered him. When he disagreed with her, she'd rejected him. "Alana Benton, you've got a lot to learn about loving a man and loving your friends," she said calmly.

Lesson one began with being able to admit she was less than perfect. She'd have learned it earlier if she'd been able to open up and admit she'd been naive and foolish when she walked into Tom Lane's dormitory room.

Lesson two built on the first lesson. She couldn't run and hide. A person who's lost always goes in circles. Alana had come full circle, right back to where she'd started. The only difference was, by running she'd compounded her problems.

Lesson three was the most difficult. A person who genuinely loved someone trusted them. It wasn't necessary to struggle to be constantly in control of everything around one.

A wry smile tugged at her lips as she wondered if she should practice making casseroles, and drinking Pepsi. Maybe those were the ingredients of humble pie.

Minutes later, she pulled into Sylas's driveway. She looked in the detached garage. His car wasn't there. She glanced at her watch. It was after five o'clock. Since she'd stormed out of his office and they weren't working on Leslie Faye's case, she wondered where he'd gone.

"It doesn't matter," she decided. "I'll camp on his doorstep until dawn, if necessary."

Sylas knocked on the front door of Leslie Faye's condominium. His heart beat faster when he heard the noise of things being slammed around inside the living room reverberating through the door.

He clenched his fist and pounded harder. "Leslie Faye! Alana! What's going on in there? Open the door."

He tried the knob. It wasn't locked. Ready to attack anyone who dared to harm either of the women, he charged through the door. He stopped abruptly when he saw Leslie Faye holding a framed picture over her head, then carelessly dropping it. Enjoyment and satisfaction were written on her face.

"I suppose she sent you over here," Leslie Faye said, smugly grinding the sole of her shoe on the broken glass. "It won't do her any good. I divorced Gregory to get his attention. By damn, I can divorce myself from Alana without legal advice from my attorney."

Sylas swung his head from left to right searching for Alana. Cardboard boxes were scattered around the room. He glanced toward the hallway and saw the attic steps scissored down from the ceiling.

"I came here to see Alana."

"She's gone," Leslie Faye said succinctly.

Although Sylas heard the triumphant note in her voice, he also saw damp streaks of mascara beneath Leslie Faye's eyes. Feeling distinctly uncomfortable, he cleared his throat and asked, "Any idea where she went?"

Leslie Faye picked a cheerleader pom-pom from the nearest box and began plucking out the plastic streamers. "I told her to go to hell, but I doubt she took my suggestion."

"Care to tell me why you're upset?"

She looked at him as though he had snakes in his hair. "I'm not upset. I'm just cleaning out the attic. It's long overdue."

"You and Alana had a quarrel?"

Leslie Faye snorted. "You might say that. And in the same breath you might say World War II was an international political rally."

"How would you describe it?"

The technique of asking open-ended questions, which Alana had taught him, wasn't wasted. Leslie Faye was being more difficult than the mythical oystacuda he'd concocted to describe Alana's behavior. He suspected Leslie Faye, not content with shredding the pom-pom, might well take a bite out of his backside for intruding on her.

"Worlds colliding...hers and mine." Her chin wobbled as she tugged at a stubborn strip of plastic. She wiped a fresh torrent of tears off her cheek by lifting her shoulder until her blouse raked against her face. "Has she told you why she left Texas years ago?"

"Do you mind if I sit down?" Sylas asked, giving himself a moment to decide how much he should confide in Leslie Faye.

"No. Just throw one of the boxes off the balcony if you can't find a place on the floor." She hiccuped loudly. "It's only junk."

Sylas had barely felt the sofa cushion touch his posterior when Leslie Faye demanded, "Has she?"

"I'm not certain I should betray a confidence."

"Don't give me that legal jargon. I was married to an attorney. I know how you guys protect your clients." Her hand muffled another hiccup. "Alana isn't your client. I am. Answer the question."

Sylas decided she deserved an honest reply. "Yes. She did."

"Great!" She tossed the stick with a few straggly pieces of streamers into the air. "She's known me forever, but I found out today. How 'bout them rotten apples?"

"She didn't want to burden you with her problems."

Leslie Faye brushed a bag off the chair nearest Sylas and crumpled into its soft cushions. "She didn't tell me because she thinks I'm a ditz."

"Ditz?"

"You know...airhead. Featherbrain. A dumb blonde."

"I can't believe that's what she told you."

"She didn't have to say it. I've always known that mentally she's a lighthouse beacon and I'm a flashlight. When we were kids she came up with the daz-

zling ideas and I came up with the ones that fizzled."
Grudgingly she added, "And when my ideas fizzled
and we got into trouble, Alana usually insisted on
taking the blame."

She folded her knees Indian style, propped her chin
in her hands and took a deep breath to end her hic-
cups. "She never needed me. She doesn't need anybody. She's proved that."

"I think she needs both of us," Sylas replied quietly. "She's lived in a world of hurt for so long,
though, I'm not certain she knows how to reach out
and ask for help. I'm scared to death she may never be
able to stop running long enough to realize how much
we both love her."

"I don't—oh hell, I love her, too," she confessed.
"I can destroy everything that reminds me of her, but
I can't tear her out of my heart." She covered her face
with her hands. "I said terrible things to her. My
mouth started rolling and I couldn't get it to stop until I dropped the Cokes off the balcony."

Sylas chuckled. "That had to be the ultimate insult."

"Don't laugh at me. Gregory didn't laugh when I
burned his boxer shorts on the front lawn. Ed Morgan didn't laugh when I beaned him with a stone fish."
She sighed. "And Alana didn't laugh when I dropped
those Cokes like water balloons. I have a wicked temper when I get angry."

"I noticed," he replied, glancing around the living
room.

"She'll never forgive me this time. She's probably
on a plane to St. Louis right now."

"Did she take her clothes?"

"Uh-uh." Another rash of uncontrollable tears cascaded from the corners of her eyes. "Sh-she picked up one letter from off the beach and walked to her car like a z-zombie."

Sylas moved over to her chair, scooped her up into his arms, put her on his lap and let her cry on his shoulder. "She'll be back."

"I don't think so." She sniffed. He gave her the handkerchief from his breast pocket. "She told me she was sorry, but I wouldn't listen. She has buckets of pride, too much to grovel. What am I going to do without her?"

Sylas wondered the same thing. He couldn't picture going to the office and not having her there. Nor could he imagine getting another night's sleep without her cuddled against him. He was a patient man, but he shifted restlessly in the chair. He had to find Alana before she retreated back into her shell.

"Harumph!"

Startled, Leslie Faye bounced on Sylas's knee. He grabbed her tightly to keep her from falling. Both of them turned to see a red-faced Gregory striding into the room.

"This is cozy. My wife and my partner," Gregory said sarcastically. "How long has this been going on?"

"Less than five minutes," Leslie Faye replied, her voice bristling with indignation. She snuggled up against Sylas as though they were long-lost lovers. "Come right in. We were just getting to the interesting part."

"Temper, temper," Sylas murmured, unlatching her arms from around his neck. "I was comforting her."

Gregory bodily swept his ex-wife into his arms. "I'd say you were doing a damned fine job of it. Mind if I take up where you left off?"

"You're jealous!" Leslie Faye chortled, her wet eyes sparkling a bright blue. "I thought you were only jealous of my friendship with Alana."

Unwilling to discuss private matters in front of his business partner, Gregory said gruffly, "Did a hurricane sweep in from the Gulf that I didn't hear about? This place is a disaster area."

"Leslie Faye and Alana had words," Sylas explained, taking back his white handkerchief, which Leslie Faye was dangling in front of her husband's nose as if it were a flag of surrender.

"About Collier's offer?"

"No." She squirmed out of his arms. "It's personal."

Gregory recognized the stubborn tilt of his wife's chin. He could badger her for the next century and she wouldn't reveal what she'd argued about with her friend until she was good and ready. He reached into his breast pocket and pulled out a folded document. "I think I have something that's going to be of interest to both of you. It's the detective's latest report."

"What's in it?" Leslie Faye unfolded the pages. "It's just lists of names and addresses."

"Names, addresses and phone numbers of the women Ed Morgan has dated during the past six months. See the asterisks? Those are women he's either attempted or successfully raped." Gregory gestured for her to give the list to Sylas. "The name at the top of the list is the woman who furnished most of the other names."

Sylas whistled between his teeth as he read the names. He asked Gregory, "How'd she get the other names?"

"She told the detective that she'd heard about Ed Morgan filing charges against Leslie Faye. She thought about what happened to her, put two and two together and decided to do a little snooping around to find out if Morgan had tried the same thing with other women. She's been following Morgan for months! She said she'd considered calling you, but she wanted to get these women's permission to use their names before she involved them. Yesterday, before our detective contacted her, she called Collier and told him that if he didn't drop the charges she was prepared to testify on Leslie Faye's behalf."

"If she's willing to go to court, why didn't she press charges at the time?" Sylas asked, beginning to understand the reason for Collier's sudden urge to settle out of court.

"She's a widow with young children. From what I can gather, she didn't want her kids to know she'd been involved with Ed. And she didn't know about the other women then. She's still hoping not to have to testify. That's why she called Collier." Gregory hugged Leslie Faye hard. "Sweetheart, I think your worries are over."

Sylas grimaced in disgust as he counted the women's names. Nine. Nine safe victims. "He belongs in jail."

"What happens now?" Leslie Faye asked Gregory.

"Sylas will contact Collier first thing in the morning about dropping charges, and then you and I are going to the marriage license bureau." He dropped a kiss on her lips. "You promised you'd give me an answer once this ordeal was finished."

Leslie Faye glanced at Sylas, then up at Gregory. "When the charges are dropped, I could file charges against Ed Morgan, couldn't I? That's what Alana wanted me to do."

"You realize you'd have to testify in open court against him, don't you?" Sylas asked, rising to his feet. "The other women may or may not be willing to come forward."

"But if one of us doesn't have the guts to do something, that list will get longer, won't it?"

"Yes." Sylas folded the list and silently gestured to Gregory for verification that he could keep the list. "I'd say he's probably not too worried about the others or he wouldn't have pressed charges against you."

Leslie Faye bit her lip as she looked up at Gregory. "You don't want me to file charges, do you?"

"I want what's best for you," Gregory replied. "It could be a nasty trial with a lot of publicity. Their only defense would be to attack your moral character."

"I don't have anything to be ashamed of." Her eyes locked with Gregory's. "I dated several men, but I never went to bed with any of them. But, frankly, even if I had, it wouldn't give Ed Morgan the right to attack me or any other woman."

"I think you two should discuss this privately," Sylas said, moving toward the front door. "Whatever you decide to do, I'm behind you one hundred percent. I'm going to start searching for Alana."

"That won't be tough," Gregory said. "I drove by your place before I came out here. Her car was in your driveway and I think I saw her on the swing on your front porch.''

''Why didn't you stop and pick her up?'' Leslie Faye asked.

''I didn't want to make you jealous,'' he teased, nibbling her ear.

She playfully swatted him on his cheek.

''I wanted to be your hero, to be the one bringing you the detective's good news. I thought it might influence your decision about marriage—in my favor.''

When Sylas heard Leslie Faye croon, ''You'll have to convince me,'' he didn't bother to say goodbye. Neither of them would have heard him.

Curled up on the swing, Alana lethargically pushed her foot against the floorboards to keep it in steady motion. Her eyes stung from crying. Her face felt stiff. Although she'd recognized her mistakes and knew what she'd have to do to set them right, she wondered if Sylas and Leslie Faye would forgive her.

The thought of leaving Galveston with both of them angry at her sent another tear sliding from the corner of her eye to her ear. She'd been alone and lonely when she left ten years ago. Fear had kept her away. Now, the knowledge that her fears had been unjustified— Tom Lane hadn't been trying to repeat that horrible episode, and Leslie Faye wouldn't have condemned her—made the prospect of going through another exile immeasurably depressing.

She could move back to Texas. Her job did give her the option of locating in one place or traveling, but she wasn't sure she could bear living in the same small city as Sylas and Leslie Faye, hovering on the fringe of

their lives. Inevitably, whether planned or un-
planned, she would bump into them. The thought of
being close enough to touch them but being rejected by
them made her feel like a kid with empty pockets
standing in the middle of a candy store.

Her fingers fiddled nervously with the corner of the
envelope she'd tucked next to her heart. She had to
garner strength from her inner reserve to give her the
tenacity to hang in there until Sylas and Leslie Faye
listened to her.

She heard a car pull into the driveway and bolted
upright. Her leg stiffened, propelling the swing backward. Off balance, momentarily dizzy, Alana clung to
the chain that dropped from the ceiling to maintain
her equilibrium.

The speeches she'd carefully rehearsed in her mind
disappeared into nothingness when she saw Sylas get
out of his car. Just the sight of him had her heart
hammering in her chest.

As he climbed the steps she rose from the swing.
"Sylas, I'm sorry," she blurted, her voice faint and
weary. It was the primary thought in her mind, the
only one that mattered.

Sylas grinned. He would have opened his arms and
patiently waited for her to come to him, but he
couldn't bear to be apart from her while she methodically gave him reasons for her apology. In two short
strides, she was in his arms and he was whirling her
around and around.

Joy flooded through Alana. She looped her arms
around his shoulders and clung tightly to him. "You
aren't angry?"

"I may be a grouch in the morning, but I don't hold a grudge," he murmured between kisses. "We're both human. We're bound to make mistakes."

His lips slanted over hers in a fiery kiss. He could taste the salt of her tears as his tongue parted her lips. Silently he swore he'd do his damnedest to keep her from being unhappy again. It seemed to him they'd both waited an eternity to find happiness.

"One promise," he said, as he lifted her fully into his arms and carried her inside.

"Anything."

She pressed her face against his shoulder and inhaled a mixed fragrance of soap, cologne and the starch in his shirt collar. She didn't deserve a man like Sylas, but maybe with his patience she could earn his love.

"You don't run away from me." He mounted the steps leading to the second floor. "I nearly went out of my mind worrying that you might vanish without a trace."

Her eyes squeezed closed. She didn't think it possible to shed another tear, but she did. Sweet tears of joy seeped through her dark lashes.

"Don't cry, sweetheart." He carefully placed her on his bed and wiped her tears. He thought of telling her about Gregory's good news, but when she opened her eyes and he saw dark flames of passion lighting them, he selfishly discarded the idea.

Impatient to feel her warmth against his skin, he began stripping her clothes away. Feverishly her fingers pushed buttons through holes, unclasped his belt buckle, unzipped his trousers. As she removed his clothes, his skin felt hot to her touch, as though a raging fever burned inside him.

They'd made love several times during the past week, but with each frenzied stroke of his hand across her breasts, stomach and thighs, she felt the hard kernel of reserve she'd still held back, finally, heatedly disintegrate. Her hands flurried over him. She felt as though the love she felt for him had turned her inside out, like Leslie Faye's sweater.

She pulled him on top of her when he would have moved onto the bed at her side. "I need you," she whispered.

Sylas groaned as her long legs wrapped around his hips and held him intimately against her. Silently he struggled to rein in his passion.

"Too fast," he mumbled, bracing his arms to roll beside her.

"No. Don't leave me," she entreated, eager to be one with him.

She arched her hips until she felt his restraint break. He thrust inside of her. Her heels pressed into the backs of his thighs until he completely filled the void she'd felt when she thought she'd lost him.

In a lover's language as old as time, she openly spoke to him of her desire, her love with each rotation and thrust of her hips. I love you, she silently chanted, then spoke the words aloud as she felt him lift her higher and higher toward the pinnacle of love. Alana's agony of desire had her straining to capture the ecstasy just out of reach.

Sylas trembled from bone through muscle and sinew to skin. He began making love to her at a pace that swirled them both outside the boundaries of reason.

"You are mine, Alana, heart and soul," he claimed hoarsely, exploding inside of her. "I'll never let you leave me."

What seemed like aeons later to Sylas, he watched Alana groggily open her eyes. Her slow recovery alarmed him. He worried that he'd frightened her by the unchecked power of his passion.

"Sweetheart, tell me I didn't hurt you," he whispered anxiously.

Alana took his hand and swept it down the length of her body. "No broken bones," she said, with a deliciously satisfied smile in her voice. "You made me tingle inside and out."

Chuckling in relief, he said, "I thought you'd fainted."

"Swooned," Alana corrected, lazily winking one eye. Her knees brushed against each other as she savored the sensations still alive within her. "Definitely a swoon, counselor."

He feathered kisses along her brow. "I'd have come home sooner if I'd known you were waiting for me."

Alana stretched to clear the fuzzy haze of lovemaking from her mind. "Where did you go looking for me?"

"The beach. I must have walked halfway from the fishing pier to the condo, searching for you."

Frowning, Alana saw an image of pictures and letters caught in the wind, strewn on the beach.

"What's the frown for?" Sylas asked, sensitive to her change of mood.

"Leslie Faye and I had a wingdinger of a fight."

"So I heard."

"We weren't shouting loud enough to be heard five miles away, were we?"

"Uh-uh. I went to the condo looking for you."

"Did she tell you I'm a lousy friend?"

"Not in so many words," Sylas replied, reluctant to step into a disagreement between two women who'd been lifelong friends. Certain Alana and Leslie Faye would heal the breach, he had to be careful of what he said.

"She came unglued when I told her why I'd left Texas." Alana moved closer to Sylas, suddenly cold. "She thinks I deserted her. Why didn't I realize how much I'd hurt her with my silence?"

"A person can only cope with a limited amount of mental anguish. After all, self-preservation is our strongest instinct. Once she's settled down, I think the two of you can work out your problem."

"Pepsi. I'm going to buy her a case of Pepsi as a peace offering."

Sylas hadn't the foggiest notion why Pepsi would make a difference.

"And tonight, I'm going to fix shrimp gumbo for you."

"Making love to you must have fatigued my mind. Is shrimp gumbo supposed to be some sort of peace offering you're making to me?"

"Uh-uh. You know, it has shrimp and rice and tomato sauce and onions and green peppers—" she took a breath "—and they're all mixed together."

"Did I hear a silent 'yuck' attached to your list of ingredients?" he teased. It pleased him to know she wanted to make such a drastic change in her eating habits just to make him happy. "I don't expect sacrifices from you. I love you just the way you are."

"Do you?"

"Hmm. Shall I prove it?"

"By arranging your food in tidy little spoonfuls on your plate?"

His hand cupped her breast; he slowly circled her nipple until it responded to his touch. "I think I have a better way in mind."

Chapter Fifteen

Here." The night chain on the door allowed only three inches for Leslie Faye to peer through. Alana held up the case of Pepsi. "I'd like mine over ice, please."

"It's a little early for soda pop, isn't it?" Leslie Faye made a valiant effort to mimic the tone of Alana's mother. "Your teeth are going to rot."

"I'd rather have rotten teeth than be a rotten friend." Her brown eyes eloquently pleaded her case. "Are you going to let me in, or am I going to sit on the balcony and drink the entire case all by myself."

"Gluttony is a sin." Leslie Faye removed the chain from the door. With a flounce of her curly head, she took the soda and said, "I wouldn't be much of a friend if I encouraged it."

Alana trailed her inside the condo. Getting in the front door was a promising sign, she thought. Leslie Faye hadn't exactly welcomed her with open arms, but then again, she hadn't thrown anything at her, either. Instead, she'd taken the soda to the kitchen.

Alana's eyes narrowed as she surveyed the mess in the living room. Automatically she stooped to pick up strings of white and purple plastic. Beneath them she saw a picture of herself and Leslie Faye in their drill uniforms, posing like glamorous Dallas Cowgirls. Seashells strewn on the floor led to Leslie Faye's prize possession in high school and college—her diary.

Alana picked it up. The strap holding the binding together had a tiny lock on it. As she put the book on the cocktail table, it fell open.

She hesitated, wondering if Leslie Faye would mind if she read it. As teenagers, they'd often given each other permission to read their diaries, but Alana felt unsure how Leslie Faye would react today.

"Turn to January eleventh. That's the day you moved out of our dorm room," Leslie Faye said behind her, handing Alana a filled glass. "Read it out loud."

Alana swallowed as she silently read the first line.

"Go on. I want you to know how I felt."

"'Dear Diary,'" she read, her voice thick with emotion. "'Alana Benton broke my heart today. She'd been acting weird. Real weird.'" Leslie Faye had underlined the last two words three times. "'I think maybe she knows about me and Gregory sleeping together.'"

Alana glanced up at Leslie Faye, who'd taken a seat on the sofa. "I don't think I should be reading this. It's private."

"I do." Leslie Faye sat on the floor next to Alana. "Yesterday I lambasted you for severing our friendship. Last night, when I read through those pages, I realized you weren't the only one who kept secrets. Go on. You have my permission."

"I don't think Gregory would approve," Alana protested. "This doesn't involve just the two of us."

Leslie Faye plucked the diary from Alana's hands. "Okay. I'll read it. Where were you?" Her finger skidded down the page. "Here we are. 'I know that when we were kids we vowed to be virgins until our wedding night, but my attitude has changed since then. Hell, I think Alana and I were the only virgins on campus! Besides, I didn't think she'd find out. I wanted to tell her about it. But, I don't know, it seemed kind of private. Something special between Gregory and me. I guess I screwed up (ha-ha). Only I'm not laughing. She didn't want me to go to the airport with her and her parents, but I insisted.'"

She looked at Alana. Her blue eyes swam in tears. Her fingers curled over Alana's hand. "When I wrote this I didn't understand why I insisted. I do now. 'I tried to hug her before she walked through the gate, but she pushed me away as though my hands would soil her dress. It broke my heart.' But it wasn't me that you thought was dirty. It was you, Alana, wasn't it? You thought what had happened could happen to me."

"It did almost happen to you, Leslie Faye. I think that's why I fainted at the airport when you told me."

She clutched Leslie Faye's hand so tightly she felt how small and fragile her friend's fingers were. "If I hadn't been too ashamed to tell you, maybe the Ed Morgan incident wouldn't have happened."

"That's ridiculous! We both know you can't tell what's going on in a man's mind just by looking at him. It could happen to any woman." She snapped the diary closed with finality. "We can't change the misunderstanding of the past. Drink your Coke."

"Pepsi," Alana corrected dryly.

"Uh-uh. Coke. After I read what I'd written in the diary, I went downstairs with a flashlight and retrieved the Cokes. The bottles that fell into the sand didn't break." Her eyes dropped to their hands, still linked together. "And the album was still there. I couldn't find most of your letters."

"They don't matter. What's important is knowing we never stopped caring about each other." Alana touched the rim of her glass against Leslie Faye's glass. "Friends?"

"Yeah. Best of friends." She grinned impishly and hooked her arm through Alana's, the way they had as kids. Then she took a long gulp of her drink. Alana did the same. "Okay, friend. I need some advice. It's about those clothes you made me buy. You know, the dresses with the Peter Pan collars."

"Take them back," Alana replied instantly, thinking how great it felt to be back on good terms with Leslie Faye. "You haven't worn them. It shouldn't be a problem."

"I may need them—and you. Did Sylas tell you what the detective discovered?"

Alana nodded. Before he'd left for the office he'd filled her in on what had happened and shown her the list. "He said you and Gregory were discussing what steps you should take."

"Gregory says it's my decision. Should I file charges against Ed Morgan? What would you do?"

"I can't decide for you. You drank Coke because it's my favorite. I don't want to influence your decision on this."

But Alana knew what she herself would do. Her dark eyes burned with the desire to see Ed Morgan brought to justice. Tom had atoned for what he'd done, but Morgan would add names to that list of abused women with regularity unless someone stopped him.

"Would you agree to work with Avery Collier?"

"He might object."

"I'd insist. I'm good at convincing lawyers how valuable your services are, remember?"

Alana nodded. "I usually work with defense attorneys, because the county governments frown on paying consultant fees, but on this case I'd do it for free. That should help you persuade Collier."

"Do you think we can put Morgan behind bars?"

"If not, I think the publicity surrounding the case will make him damned unattractive to the women around here." She hated to throw a wet blanket on Leslie Faye's plans, but she had to ask, "Do you realize that you'll be part of that publicity?"

Leslie Faye grimaced. "I'm not a martyr. But I know I'd feel guilty if I heard about another woman being victimized. You kept quiet because you were nineteen and scared and ashamed. My knees will be knocking together, but I'm not ashamed anymore. Like I said, this can happen to any woman."

"Did I ever tell you I'm proud to call you friend?" Alana asked sincerely.

"Once." Leslie Faye chuckled. "When I took the blame for putting sand crabs in Felicia Taylor's desk."

Alana laughed. "Well, you did have a problem—what with my being absent from school that day."

"You helped me catch the crabs, though," Leslie Faye countered, pretending to be indignant.

"We were going to use them as bait for surf fishing."

"Sure we were," Leslie Faye replied sarcastically. "But I remember what you wanted to do with the stinky fish."

"Okay! Felicia wasn't our favorite person. I admit it!"

Leslie Faye giggled as she bounded to her feet. "I think we ought to drop by the office right away. Gregory will be sitting on pins and needles wondering what I'm going to do next." Her eyes sparkled with mischief. "It's good for him. Keeps him from thinking his law books are more exciting than I am."

Sylas gave the thumbs-up signal to Gregory as he hung up the phone. "Collier thinks he can convince Morgan to drop the charges."

"What did he say when you mentioned the possibility of Leslie Faye pressing charges?"

"Well, I have to give the man credit for being able to eat humble pie and sing 'The Star Spangled Banner' at the same time. I believe his exact words were, 'I want to pursue justice for every citizen of Galveston County,' which translates into 'Morgan made me look foolish.' In Texas lingo, he wants to kick butt and take names. Leslie Faye and I are supposed to take the list of women's names to him as soon as it's convenient for her.''

"Great!'' Gregory glanced at the stacks of material on date rape on Sylas's desk. "I guess you won't be needing more lessons on jury selection. Did Alana happen to mention when she'd be leaving for St. Louis?''

"We didn't discuss it.'' Sylas leveled his eyes on Gregory as his partner started to get up from his chair. "I've been thinking about our partnership, Gregory. It's time to expand our horizons.''

"Oh, no.'' He raised both hands, palms toward Sylas. "Alana and I are on friendly terms for the first time in a decade, but our partnership doesn't require the services of a jury consultant. If you want to retain her, then offer her another type of partnership.''

"Such as?''

"Marriage.''

"You're recommending marriage?'' Sylas scoffed. "I seem to remember you saying that any man who considered marriage ought to be required by law to have a frontal lobotomy.''

Sylas couldn't resist tweaking Gregory's nose. He felt confident Leslie Faye had accomplished the objective she'd had in mind when she divorced Gregory to get his attention. And he himself had given serious thought to proposing to Alana, but in case he'd overrated her attraction to him, he wanted to keep her in Galveston by offering her a job.

"I'm crazy," Gregory admitted good-naturedly. "Crazy in love with my wife. I've proposed to her a dozen times. She doesn't say yes and she doesn't say no. She just gives me one of her flirty winks and asks me about my caseload. The woman is driving me totally bonkers!"

"Alana mentioned several law firms in St. Louis that would be interested in my qualifications," Sylas fibbed. "You know the old saying about Mohammed and the mountain."

"That's blackmail," Gregory roared. "Damned troublemaker! I told you—"

"Yes?" Leslie Faye answered, bursting into the office and plopping herself on Gregory's lap. "Did you call my name?"

Alana followed her into the room at a sedate pace. The smile Sylas gave her warmed her heart. She'd never admit it, but the thought of staying in Galveston to work with Avery Collier held special appeal when she thought of being with Sylas.

"No, love," Gregory replied, glancing from Sylas to Alana, watching as Sylas pulled up a chair for Alana and seated her close to the corner of the desk. Peeved by his partner's defection to his ex-archenemy's camp, he turned his attention to Leslie Faye and dropped a kiss on her upturned lips. "We were discussing business. Collier has agreed to drop charges. He wants you and Sylas to come by his office."

"Did you blackmail Collier?" Leslie Faye asked.

"Uh-uh." He glanced at Sylas in time to catch sight of Sylas reaching for Alana's hand. "Sylas is blackmailing me into making Alana a partner."

Leslie Faye gave Gregory a cheeky grin. "Don't worry, honey, I think Alana has other plans."

"Do you?" Sylas asked, his heart skipping a beat in fear of hearing she'd made plane reservations while at Leslie Faye's condo.

"Unless Gregory objects, I plan on donating my services to Avery Collier on the case of the state versus Ed Morgan." The dirty look Sylas gave Gregory made Alana wonder what Sylas was holding over his partner to put pressure on him. Unwanted pressure, she mused, feeling perfectly capable of locating clients without help from either man. "Do you have a problem with my working with the prosecuting attorney?"

Leslie Faye replied pointedly, "That's my case. Gregory knows I'm able to decide who and what I want. Right, dear?"

"I make the big decisions, like should we send a man to Mars, and she makes the little decisions, like setting our wedding date," Gregory said, chuckling at his wife's spunkiness. "And speaking of weddings, since Alana is going to be in Galveston and you want her to be your bridesmaid, you could take pity on a poor, miserable bachelor and make an honest man of me."

Alana hid a smile behind the hand Sylas wasn't holding as she observed Leslie Faye pretending to consider his proposal.

"Sylas will be my best man," Gregory promised as further enticement. "It's what you always wanted."

"Now wait a minute," Sylas interrupted. He took a deep breath and said, "I vowed never to be the best man in someone else's wedding again. This time, I'm going to be simply the best, period!" He lifted the back of Alana's hand to his lips. "What do you think of double weddings?"

"Fabulous idea," Leslie Faye squealed, enthusiastically hugging Gregory.

Alana thought so, too, but she wasn't going to be stampeded into making a decision. Sylas might regret his spur-of-the-moment proposal. Taking a lesson from her friend, she answered, "I'll think about it."

"Uh-oh," Leslie Faye groaned. She grabbed Gregory by the hand and jumped to her feet. "I think this is where you and I make a hasty exit. He's going to have to convince her."

Anxious to get a firm commitment from her, Gregory said, "Lead the way, woman. I'm right behind you."

"That's where I plan on keeping you, too," Leslie Faye teased, fluffing her curls. She sashayed seductively to the door with Gregory close on her heels. Leaving the room without giving a final word of advice was beyond her. With the wink of an eye, she said, "You'd better snap up this offer, ol' buddy. Spinsterhood is just around the corner and we both know he is the best man for you."

As Gregory started to close the door behind them, he added, "Go ahead and throw in a partnership offer if that sweetens the pot. Leslie Faye is liable to whack me over the head with a two-by-four if I place a stumbling block in the path of true love."

After Gregory's surrender—none too gracious, Sylas thought—and when they were alone, he tugged on Alana's hands until he'd pulled her on his lap. Afraid he'd prejudiced her against the idea of marrying him by proposing in front of Gregory and Leslie Faye, he asked, "Are you angry with me?"

"No."

"Scared of making a lifetime commitment?"

"No." She teased the fullness of his bottom lip with her forefinger while her skin tingled from the touch of his hand brushing her hair back from her face. "When I'm angry and scared, I run."

"I'm hoping you'll run straight into my arms from here on in." He brushed his mouth against hers gently. Once. Twice. Wanting to linger, but needing a direct answer to his proposal, he continued, "I want to marry you, Alana. If my timing was off, I apologize. Should I get down on bended knee?"

Alana shook her head, desiring more than gentle kisses. "Bad body language. It denotes a willingness to let a woman dominate the relationship. I'm in favor of equality."

He teased her mouth with the tip of his tongue. "It's a Victorian gesture. Back then it was the only time a man let a woman dominate him. But, I'm willing to propose again, standing toe-to-toe."

Her lips parted. A horizontal position, lying side by side, she mused, was more along the line of where his seductive powers were taking her. She sipped at his tongue, drawing him inside of her.

The tiny voice in the back of her mind that had been mute since she'd laid eyes on Sylas blared, "Go for the gold ring!"

Methodically, she began to unloosen his tie. Two could play his game of seducing the response he wanted. She neatly folded the tie and placed it on his desk.

"You can't have your way with me before you give me an answer," Sylas warned, loving the bright glow in her dark eyes. In an orderly fashion, she unbuttoned his shirt to his waist. He clamped his hands on the arms of the chair to keep them from touching her. "I'm a patient man. I know you could spend weeks weighing the pros and cons of marriage. But I'd like to make a suggestion."

"What?"

"Weigh them after the honeymoon, would you? On this one issue I'm damned impatient."

She strung a line of kisses across the thick mat of dark hair on his chest. "I might consider a double wedding, but I passionately refuse to go on a double honeymoon with Leslie Faye and Gregory."

"Coercion is illegal," he groaned as her tongue flicked over his flat male nipple. Where she got the idea he'd agree to such a preposterous idea he didn't know. "No double honeymoon."

"That's the next thing Leslie Faye will come up with," she said, softly laughing as his hair tickled her nose. "I just thought I'd warn you."

"Stop warning me. Just say you'll marry me."

Prolonging the delightful torment as long as possible, she said, "And I don't want Gregory blackmailed into taking me into the partnership."

"It's the only way I could think of to keep you here." He leaned forward to let her strip off his shirt, then clamped his hands on her hips to keep them from squirming against him. "For God's sake, woman, don't fold the damned thing. I've got another one in my bottom drawer in case of an emergency."

"Will my neat and tidy attitudes drive you crazy?"

"I adore neat and tidy," he groaned between clenched teeth, sucking in his stomach while she unbuckled his belt.

A sharp rap on the door stilled Alana's bold fingers.

"Have you convinced her yet?" Leslie Faye called through the closed door.

"No!" Sylas shouted. "Don't come in here! And tell Carmela to hold my calls!"

"You're going to have wait a little longer, Gregory. My heart is set on a double wedding. You know, I've been thinking. Alana and I always wanted to go to scuba diving for shipwrecked treasure."

Alana rolled her eyes heavenward. "No, Leslie Faye. No double honeymoon."

She opened the bottom drawer of the desk with her toe. Once Leslie Faye started pestering them Alana knew she'd continue interrupting them until she got the answer she wanted. Alana slid off Sylas's lap and shot a dirty look toward the door. "I told you she'd come up with a crazy idea, didn't I?"

"Gregory may be right about a man needing a frontal lobotomy before walking down the aisle," Sylas groaned. He took the shirt Alana handed him. "I have a gut feeling the dynamic duo is about to become the frustrated foursome if we don't get out of here."

"Yeah."

She reached for the box of tissues on his desk to wipe the traces of lipstick from his mouth.

Sylas caught her hand. "She said yes," he shouted, then chuckled softly.

Her chuckle mingled joyfully with his when they both heard Leslie Faye gave a Texas-size whoop of delight.

"I said yes, meaning we should get out of here," Alana whispered. Deciding Leslie Faye would bodily block their leaving if Alana didn't give Sylas an answer, she added, "I'd love being your wife."

"She said yes again," Sylas shouted. He shrugged into the clean shirt. His eyes twinkled with mirth as he added loudly, "I think she wants to elope."

"Alana Benton!" The door burst open. Arms flailing, Leslie Faye stomped into the room. "That's the meanest thing you could do, Alana Benton. If you think I'm going to let you cheat yourself out of a big wedding with all the trimmings, you can just find yourself another friend!"

Gregory swept Leslie Faye into his arms and stifled her tirade by kissing her as he carried her back toward his office. Sylas grabbed Alana's elbow to hurry her down the hall.

Once outside, Sylas pulled Alana into his arms. "I love you, Alana-soon-to-be-Kincaid."

She lifted her face, letting the hot Texas sun and his love warm her. She could almost feel her roots sinking back into the island's sand. Her self-imposed exile was over. She was home in his arms.

"I love you, Sylas Kincaid. You are ... simply the best."

* * * * *

SILHOUETTE'S "BIG WIN"
SWEEPSTAKES RULES & REGULATIONS
NO PURCHASE NECESSARY TO ENTER OR RECEIVE A PRIZE

1. To enter and join the Reader Service, scratch off the metallic strips on all your BIG WIN tickets #1–#6. This will reveal the values for each sweepstakes entry number, the number of free book(s) you will receive, and your free bonus gift as part of our Reader Service. If you do not wish to take advantage of our Reader Service, but wish to enter the Sweepstakes only, scratch off the metallic strips on your BIG WIN tickets #1–#4. Return your entire sheet of tickets intact. Incomplete and/or inaccurate entries are ineligible for that section or sections of prizes. Not responsible for mutilated or unreadable entries or inadvertent printing errors. Mechanically reproduced entries are null and void.

2. Whether you take advantage of this offer or not, your Sweepstakes numbers will be compared against a list of winning numbers generated at random by the computer. In the event that all prizes are not claimed by March 31, 1992, a random drawing will be held from all qualified entries received from March 30, 1990 to March 31, 1992, to award all unclaimed prizes. All cash prizes (Grand to Sixth), will be mailed to the winners and are payable by cheque in U.S. funds. Seventh prize to be shipped to winners via third-class mail. These prizes are in addition to any free, surprise or mystery gifts that might be offered. Versions of this sweepstakes with different prizes of approximate equal value may appear in other mailings or at retail outlets by Torstar Corp. and its affiliates.

3. The following prizes are awarded in this sweepstakes: ★ Grand Prize (1) $1,000,000; First Prize (1) $35,000; Second Prize (1) $10,000; Third Prize (5) $5,000; Fourth Prize (10) $1,000; Fifth Prize (100) $250; Sixth Prize (2500) $10; ★★ Seventh Prize (6000) $12.95 ARV.

   ★ This Sweepstakes contains a Grand Prize offering of $1,000,000 annuity. Winner will receive $33,333.33 a year for 30 years without interest totalling $1,000,000.

   ★★ Seventh Prize: A fully illustrated hardcover book published by Torstar Corp. Approximate value of the book is $12.95.

   Entrants may cancel the Reader Service at any time without cost or obligation to buy (see details in center insert card).

4. This promotion is being conducted under the supervision of Marden-Kane, Inc., an independent judging organization. By entering this Sweepstakes, each entrant accepts and agrees to be bound by these rules and the decisions of the judges, which shall be final and binding. Odds of winning in the random drawing are dependent upon the total number of entries received. Taxes, if any, are the sole responsibility of the winners. Prizes are nontransferable. All entries must be received by no later than 12:00 NOON, on March 31, 1992. The drawing for all unclaimed sweepstakes prizes will take place May 30, 1992, at 12:00 NOON, at the offices of Marden-Kane, Inc., Lake Success, New York.

5. This offer is open to residents of the U.S., the United Kingdom, France and Canada, 18 years or older except employees and their immediate family members of Torstar Corp., its affiliates, subsidiaries, Marden-Kane, Inc., and all other agencies and persons connected with conducting this Sweepstakes. All Federal, State and local laws apply. Void wherever prohibited or restricted by law. Any litigation respecting the conduct and awarding of a prize in this publicity contest may be submitted to the Régie des loteries et courses du Québec.

6. Winners will be notified by mail and may be required to execute an affidavit of eligibility and release which must be returned within 14 days after notification or, an alternative winner will be selected. Canadian winners will be required to correctly answer an arithmetical skill-testing question administered by mail which must be returned within a limited time. Winners consent to the use of their names, photographs and/or likenesses for advertising and publicity in conjunction with this and similar promotions without additional compensation.

7. For a list of major winners, send a stamped, self-addressed envelope to: WINNERS LIST, c/o MARDEN-KANE, INC., P.O. BOX 701, SAYREVILLE, NJ 08871. Winners Lists will be fulfilled after the May 30, 1992 drawing date.

If Sweepstakes entry form is missing, please print your name and address on a 3"×5" piece of plain paper and send to:

In the U.S.	In Canada
Silhouette's "BIG WIN" Sweepstakes	Silhouette's "BIG WIN" Sweepstakes
901 Fuhrmann Blvd.	P.O. Box 609
P.O. Box 1867	Fort Erie, Ontario
Buffalo, NY 14269-1867	L2A 5X3

Offer limited to one per household.

LTY-S790RR

Diana Palmer's fortieth story for Silhouette . . . chosen as an Award of Excellence title!

CONNAL
Diana Palmer

Next month, Diana Palmer's bestselling LONG, TALL TEXANS series continues with CONNAL. The skies get cloudy on C. C. Tremayne's home on the range when Penelope Mathews decides to protect him—by marrying him!

One specially selected title receives the Award of Excellence every month. Look for CONNAL in August at your favorite retail outlet . . . only from Silhouette Romance.

.CON-1